Pride's Landing

GERALD "JERRY" ADAMS

Paperback ISBN: 978-1-958895-40-5
Digital ISBN: 978-1-958895-58-0

Contents

PROLOGUE

Puffing ebony smoke, white steam billowing out, the one car train began to brake and timed it exact with the deck connected to the new station in New London. The Alabama boys got off together and waiting were two cadre N.C.O.'s who began barking orders directing them to a bus. Loading on they sat silent with their meager bags and cases.

Billy Ray's name was called and was directed to get on a jeep that would carry him to officer training billets. He looked back at the bus as the jeep was leaving and took a large gulp. As they say back home in Alabama he'd "spoiled" them by taking care of their needs even back to the days of being "concrete finishers" while they worked together building Wilson Dam on the majestic Tennessee river.

It was almost like a mother taking her child for his first day of school. He turned and looked forward, did a silent prayer and immediately had the impression that all of them were in God's hands and even if they were grown men, he would take care of all of them now. Today they began a new life.

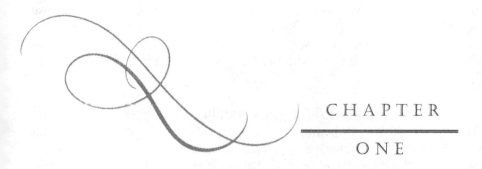

CHAPTER

ONE

The fall of nineteen forty -one, brought sounds from the breezes whistling through the boughs on the banks of the majestic Tennessee river, like a harpsichord. Billy Ray Coleman, educated at Florence Normal College, orphan Chickasaw, native Alabamian, and the pilot of the U. S. Postal sailing skiff, had just shoved off from McFarland Bottom near Florence, Alabama and would go west on the river until he reached the small village of Waterloo, the jumping place on the trail of tears. He would deliver mail to the many farmers that owned property on the north bank in Lauderdale County and after spending the night at his last stop, would cross over to the South bank in Colbert County.

Traveling with him, normally, was his Jack Russell dog named "Lucy". She was the most intelligent animal he'd ever met. She knew the stops down and back and the people knew her too.

Most of the time, if they needed a "tug". She barked loud enough to alert the upstream boats, and they would toss a rope. Lucy would jump in the river, "mouth" the pull rope and swim back to Billy Ray, who would tie it to the aft "O" ring. They would swing back and forth as the mail was delivered or picked up. Weather bad, they would pull in to selected piers and wait it out. Final stop was "Pride's Landing", an old riverboat, turn-around, and the home port for Billy Ray and Lucy. From there Billy Ray would collect mail going out and anything else that needed to be turned in at the Post Office and finish the day.

He only worked the river three days a week and took the off days and attended college. He'd already graduated with his undergraduate

1

degree but was pushing for his master's business degree.

Billy Ray had friends that he'd worked with when they were younger and had jobs building Wilson Dam as concrete finishers. Those friends now lived on the river bank and spent most of their time hunting, fishing, and trapping. Local school administrator sent teachers at various times to teach these men to take the GED test and earn their high-school diploma. So far none had done it but at least they tried.

He'd been involved for years with his school sweetheart, Gloria Norton. A beauty with beautiful blue eyes, blond hair and a figure that women envied, and men enjoyed looking at. Plans made for years concerning marriage had escalated recently and Billy Ray, an orphan, had learned early to be frugal and with great advice in investing his hard-earned salary, had been thinking about buying land so that they could build a house on property near "Pride's Landing". Gloria was ready now. She too had a good job, working as the administrative assistant to the Colbert County probate judge. Both young people were admired and enjoyed friendship from both older citizens and their colleagues from their community.

It seemed to most that they could do no wrong. Billy Ray, strongly admired and respected, had a jealous streak when it came to his "love" and she was almost as bad when her girl-friends talked of the handsome features of her "beau".

Gloria lived with her grandparents, owned her car, attended the Baptist church and associated with the gentry of their community. Billy Ray, lived at "Pride's Landing" with the family that had adopted him as a child and received counseling from his mentors. Bud, a world war one veteran, and a graduate of the University of Alabama, had lost his wife, Lily, to breast cancer early in their marriage and hadn't remarried but dated a wonderful lady named Jane, who was Billy Ray's feminine counselor or as he put it, his "Mother figure".

Several times, they double dated and never stopped using their fabulous sense of humor together. Coming up was a concert/dance at the local entertainment building known as the "Bloody Bucket", named this, due to the fist fights that occurred there on occasion. Trying to make this dance to be calm and sensible, local politicians were sponsoring known musicians and singers to promote entertainment and not "barroom" fisticuffs.

Local volunteers had cleaned the building and painted the bathrooms. A group of young ladies from the YWCA, in Memphis were in-route to Birmingham, for volleyball tournament and would spend the night in Tuscumbia and Sheffield. They had been invited to attend the concert/dance and would provide much needed dance partners.

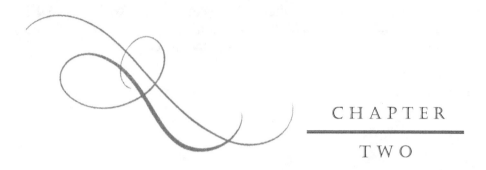

CHAPTER

TWO

The wonderful duo of man and dog, arrived in Waterloo late in the day and waiting on them was the owner of Bob's Grocery and Fuel station, Bobby Brewer. They had been friends for many years and each had great respect for the other. Brewer was an enigma. While as backwoods as many residents of the area, he carried with him an insatiable appetite for the academia arena, and never stopped quizzing Billy Ray about his college subjects. On this evening, he'd planned to seek more information on the events occurring in Europe and especially of the Nazi movement. Keeping up with the world's current events had always been a way of life that Billy Ray felt very important. Perhaps it was because he was an orphan, or poor, or his ancestry, that propelled him to ascertain daily what was occurring in other lands.

Going back upstream making deliveries was a hard way of work. He needed to use his twin Sears and Roebuck outboard motors more unless he caught a gulf-stream breeze or had no mail to deliver on the Colbert county (south) side, whereby he could "hook" up with an upstream barge making deliveries to T. V. A. In any event, he'd need to spend the night at the camp he used near the defunct village of Riverton. He'd pick up supplies for his friends that lived on the shores of "Pride's Landing". This is where he'd grown up and only there did he have a complete feeling of home.

Never tired of telling the story of how the people who lived there remained in love, respected and admired their ways of making a good life for their families. Bobby Brewer, who knew a lot of area history, asked

Billy Ray to tell him the history, again and again. Being a businessman, he especially was interested in learning how John Pride made so much money. The story had many details, but Billy Ray kept it simple as told it this way:

The Pride, Goodloe, and Harris families settled in West Colbert county from North Carolina, when they learned the Chickasaw, Cherokee and a few Choctaw, owned properties in this area and would be repositioned, therefore they settled monetarily with the Federal government. When the land opened for sale, the North Carolinians took advantage and purchased many acres. Some for plantation use, some for hunting and some for timber rights. As most land owners of that era knew, slavery was much needed to settle, bringing into the area several negro families. John Pride purchased the area near the inlet just below his cliff home and upon completing the homes for all families, he built a very large wharf for loading and unloading steamboats. Those boats, due to the shoals-rapids, had to turn around and go back stream toward Memphis, Tennessee. To do commercial business, and to the fact he was wise enough to erect the wharfs, he added a railroad spur on his property, started a ferry service connecting Colbert and Lauderdale counties and pushed for more passenger services. Near the tracks, he built facilities for the passengers, sold tickets for the railroad, and stored products dropped off by the steamboats. He expanded his lands and raised all types of livestock. His brother Hock, purchased land on the mountain-side, that was primarily used for hunting and timber. It was erroneously named "Hawk" Pride mountain rather than "Hock" Pride mountain.

Thanksgiving was fast approaching, so Billy Ray needed to alert his friends that lived on the banks of "Pride's" Landing about upcoming events and to bring them various snacks and items that made them happier. He'd picked them up at Bob Brewer's store, just before he crossed the now much wider Tennessee river as opposed to the size it once was. The gigantic Wilson Dam that T.V. A. had built; for generating electricity, was the reason the river was now over a mile wide in places. Billy Ray and Lucy did in fact spend the night at their favorite campsite. Next day they hugged the south bank and dropped off and picked up mail for distribution. They pulled into the wharf at Pride's Landing and were greeted by his old cronies: Doughbelly, Monkey, Spider, Pepper, Little Red, Rex, Eddie, and Bones.

"Whatcha got for me Billy Ray", asked Doughbelly?

"Sackfill of jaw-breakers, chewin tabackky, potted meat, and sody-crackers; answered Billy Ray with a smile on his face. Trying to emulate the colloquialism of the area."

"Well what 'bout me"? questioned Bones.

"Nuttin but fattin stuff. Peanut Butter, crackers, vienni sausages and a whole poke of candies."

"Leavin me out?" asked Spider.

"Nope, licorice sticks, nanners, coffee, sugar, and a lot 'o "loaf" bread. Now, ya'll can pull out of the box, souse meat, boloney, hot dogs, buns, tater chips, and a bunch of sweets and milk. Now guys, don't forget, this Sunday is Thanksgiving and the church will bring ya'll ham, turkey, chicken dressing, green beans, mashed potatoes, yams, and a whole bunch of cakes and Ples. In addition to the snacks I brought you, there is another box filled with soap, toilet paper, talcum powder, towels, wash rags, tooth powder, tooth brushes, and smell-'um-good stuff. Bud Goodloe will bring down some clothes for you to change into because next Saturday, there is going to be a big show and dance at the "Bloody Bucket". Sally Belle, the Confederate Flag Band, and 'ol Johnson-Grass will be playing and singing. New guy by the name of Hank Williams, from Montgomery, is heading up to Nashville and will stop off to entertain us.

Now get this! Group of gals from Memphis YWCA are on their way to Birmingham and will lay-over for the night and they have been invited to come a dance awhile. Great chance for ya'll to meet them. So, clean up, change your clothes, brush your snaggle teeth, gather about a dollar or at least seventy-five cents and be there at six o'clock. Can catch the 4:48 for Tuscumbia. Don't know how you'll get home, except get that old Reo truck fired up and drive it back and forth instead of tramping the 4:48. Up to ya'll though.

"Kin we get some work loadin up a boxcar at the spur so's we can raise the dance money"? asked Eddie.

"Don't know. Ask the loading foreman this week. But be on the dock area early next week to find out".

After storing the skiff, Lucy and Billy Ray loaded up in his truck and took the mailbag to the Post-Office in Tuscumbia for distribution.

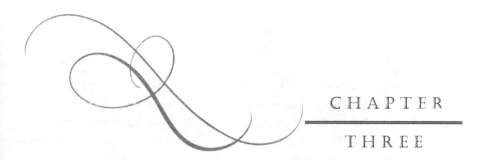

CHAPTER

THREE

Billy Ray was one of the most respected young men in Northwest Alabama. Raised since he was eleven years old by his mentor, Bud Goodloe, at a lovely location on the Tennessee river; named Pride's Landing . Story as he'd been taught from his extended family taught him that the family had lived on the river for generations and the story went: The Chickasaw and the Cherokee had inhabited this area since early last century. Upon the movement of tribal removals this area was put up for sale and the families of Pride, Goodloe, and Harris, purchased most of the land. John Pride and his brother Hoch, bought most of the land where the steamboats were forced to turn around due to the shoals. An inlet gave the boats to turn around and go back- stream toward Memphis.

They built a wharf and where to off-load passengers and mercantile there. Realizing money could be made. They petitioned the railroad to build a line including a spur and commerce expanded. Two ferries connecting to Lauderdale county opened trade for the passenger and merchandise trade. South of the wharf, Hock's land provided timber plus hunting lands. Strangest story about Hock was that his land upon being surveyed was named by accident by the surveyors as "Hawk-Pride" mountains and lands.

"Money was made by the families that resided there in great amounts, but more importantly, many jobs were invented."

Bud had not only provided a home for Billy Ray, but advised him to get a college education, helped him to land jobs, and counseled on how to invest his money and time.

Gloria too, was an orphan. Her parents left her with her maternal grandparents during the early days of the depression and sought jobs in California. However, somewhere in Texas, they were lost; and never heard from again.

She was diligently and lovingly raised by those grandparents but sorely missed her parents. In school was very popular and her looks drew people to her. Good student but lack of money kept her from attending college. Church was her main social event and accepted place. All was well until she turned the corner of upper floor at Deshler High School in Tuscumbia, Alabama, and looked in the green eyes of Billy Ray Coleman.

Perhaps it was love at first sight, but he'd had a crush on her since he saw her playing on the playground during elementary school.

Tonight, would be special night for them. They would go to the Thanksgiving dance at the Bloody Bucket double dating with Jane and Bud. But that night the specialty was he was going to officially propose to her. They had spoken about marriage many times, but nothing hard core. This would be the night. Of course, he was going to play her a long for a while and then pop the question.

Walking in a little late, they heard the western swing band of "Big" Huey and the Confederate Flag Band. Sally Belle was due next singing many new songs including Gloria's favorite, "Faded Love". The new singer from Georgiana, Alabama, Hank Williams would be up next to finish the concert.

It was a joyous evening and after the show and intermission, the band began again playing dance music. Dance floor was full. The ladies from Memphis and the guys from Tuscumbia and" Pride's Landing", mixed it up quiet-well. Naturally Gloria and Billy Ray danced very close and she whispered in his ear, "when are we going to get married Billy Ray"? Jokingly, he replied "But honey I must get another job to make enough money to buy us a house". She grinned up and said, "But honey, I want to start having BABIES.
"He spoke up laughing and said BABIES"?
"Yes", she said.

At that point, someone tapped him on his shoulder as if cutting in on the dance. He turned around and sure enough there standing behind him was a very big country boy. "cutting in city boy" he said with a smirk. "Sorry my friend but she's spoken for" answered Billy Ray. "Ya mean ya'll are hitched"? "No friend, not yet, but we were discussing it when you tapped in."

Country boy was agitated and the smirk got larger when he said, "Well, first of all; I ain't yore friend, and now you got to get out of my way before I break your neck".

With that, he shoved Billy Ray as if he was a "bully". Then he grabbed Gloria and pulled her tight to him in a very close way. After Billy Ray fell, the country boy began dancing away from the prostrate foe.

He arose as a Phoenix, with fire and strength in his muscles. He hit the country boy with such strength that the large man was knocked out immediately. Gloria screamed and two of the friends of the fellow he hit with his fist, turned and was hit on the top of his head with a Coca-Cola bottle by one of them. This knocked Billy Ray unconscious and he too hit the floor.

In his darkness, he didn't see or was aware of the brawl break out between the local guys and those from across the river from Franklin county. It took a long time to placate the fighters. Some were taken to hospital and many arrested.

Bud escorted the ladies out and took them home. Billy Ray was taken to the emergency room and was patched up. He bailed the guys from Pride's Landing out of the city and county jails.

It was Sunday morning, December 6, 1940 when he woke up with an enormous headache. It was cold, windy, but had plenty sunshine creeping into his bedroom. Rays leaked through the slats of the venetian blinds on his face. He pulled himself up and sat on the edge of the bed.

He felt the bandage on his head and began suffering the headache. After a few minutes, he arose, put his clothes on, and went into the bathroom where he washed the dry blood from his face and neck. While washing his face, he noticed and felt a very large bump on his head. Boy,

9

did it hurt he thought. He stumbled into the kitchen and took a seat at the kitchen table. He looked around the room but didn't see anyone. He could smell coffee brewing then poured himself a cup.

He searched around for some St. Joseph aspirin to aid him to alleviate the pain.
Out of nowhere, Jane came into the room.
"Morning' you thug, how are you feeling'."
"Can't get aspirin opened."
"Here, let me help you."
She opened her large purse and found a bottle. Opened, pulled a large amount of cotton from the mouth, dumped out two pills and gave them to him. While he sipped some of the coffee, she got him some cold water. He then took the pills and drank the refreshing water.

"Drink your coffee, got some news for you," Jane said.
"Is it bad" he asked.
"Yes, but it doesn't include anything that happened last night".
She had prepared an ice bag and placed it on his head, while she told him the news he'd been waiting on.
"Billy Ray, the Japanese bombed Pearl Harbor in Hawaii. We are going to war. The President has been on the radio giving the news.
He said, "in Hawaii, a lot of men were killed. "The report went.
"Where is Bud?"
"Gone with Rex to get your car."
"Where is Gloria?"
"We took her home last night. She called askin' about you. Told her you were okay, and you had a goose head on your hard head."

He finished his coffee and walked down the hill to see the "boys". He wanted their information as to what happened last -night and he wanted to tell them about what the Japanese had done.

Approaching them with fear. On the path going down to the shore was a large limestone rock. This was his personal prayer altar and today he must use it. "Lord forgive me for the way I acted last night. Now Lord teach me why a non-Christian country can kill so many in a Christian country. Will you reveal this to me? Am I not one of yours? You've loved and blessed me for all my life. Do you choose me to represent you? Do you want me to enter the military-service for my country? Regardless of my feelings Lord, I know you'll direct me. My brain isn't large enough to understand what is happening now. I'll respect and love you for what you'll do.

Lord please love and protect my family, Gloria, and the men I'm about to tell this horrid news to. Let me advise them as to defending their country. Give me wisdom oh! Lord. Hear my prayer, please...amen

"Mornin' guys, how are ya'll?" Billy Ray asked.

"Good Billy Ray, but the question is, how are you?" said Doughbelly.

Sheepishly he grinned,

"Okay, gotta headache. Can ya'll tell me what happened last night?"

"Some big 'ol boy from out on the mountain was drunk and decided he wanted to take Gloria from you. He hit you on the head with a blackjack, kinda making you a bit goofy. You then knocked him out. After that, his buddies came up and hit you on the head again but this time it was a Coca-Cola bottle. Knocking you out. After that we jumped in and beat them up. The law then entered and started hitting all of us. Didn't hurt much. We got back at them, Bones vomited in their back floorboards. And get this: Gloria jumped on the boy that hit you with the Coke bottle and nearly scratched his eyes out."

They all laughed at that.

"Ya'll gather around closer, got some news that is tragic. This morning, the Japanese bombed and attacked Pearl Harbor. That's in Hawaii. A lot of American guys were killed. I'm sure the President has declared war. On the way down, to talk to you, I stopped and prayed at the Rock.

"I feel I've been directed to join the Navy. Going in the morning to sign up. If ya'll want to do the same, catch the 9:28 freight and I'll meet you at the City café. I'll buy the coffee there. Then we'll go on to the court house to enlist. That's all. What do ya'll think."

"Billy Ray, why the Navy" asked Pepper.

"Well, it's this way: been in a boat on either a river or a creek all of my life."

"You've been in the woods all of your life also. Seems to me you'd prefer the Army" asked Monkey

"Nope"

The men looked around and talked among themselves. The decision was made unanimously to go with Billy Ray to the Navy.

"Well then, I'm going up to the house and get your birth certificates and I'll have them in the morning. Gotta go to talk to Bud now. Jane has told him, I'm sure. Tell Rex when he gets back what we've talked and decided on.

He walked up the hill to the big house and along the way, did a prayer of thanksgiving.

Bud returned with his car. Rex took it down to the landing site and washed it "sparkling clean". Bud approached Billy Ray and asked, "Did you hear the news"?

"Yes"

"What do you think?"

"Appears we're going to war. The fellas and I are joining the Navy tomorrow. Before I leave for training, I'll clear everything up with the post office. Mail I'm sure will increase so adjustments will be made. If I wait around, for sure I'll be drafted. "

"You sure about joining?"

"Yep"

'Well get with me before you go."

"Will do. Are you going to get activated?"

"Probably will. The Governor will request that I stay here and aide him."

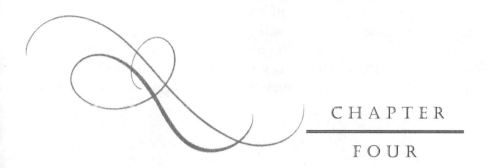

CHAPTER

FOUR

Bud had warned Billy Ray about "Big" Shine, who ran the bait shop located on the north bank half-way between the dam and the river bridge. Mr. Shine would tell anyone what was going on even if wasn't the truth. He had bought a lot of land from TVA just before the big depression occurred and he thought this entitled him to declare that he also owned the river.

Billy Ray remembered when he began his job with the post office delivering mail along the river, he was warned to stay away from Mr. Gabby Shine as much as possible due to his contacts with a lot of shady characters. Money laundering, gambling, and bootlegging, had all been linked to him. How much was true no one knew for sure.

"Big" as he liked to be known, had a slightly autistic son called "Little Shine". A story told to him, was not long after "Big" returned home from World War one, he married his long-time sweetheart, Sarah.

He got a job working for the State forestry division. Sarah and Gabby were extremely happy, especially after they bought a Victorian house on Tombigbee street in Florence. Sarah became pregnant and was thrilled when she learned there was a possibility she would deliver twins. Somehow during her pregnancy though, some type of poison entered her body. The twin boys, "Chip" and "Chuck", were delivered dead. Sarah sank into depths of depression unlike any one had ever seen. Gabby figured to get her out of the depression, getting her pregnant again was the answer. And it did, for a while. She

13

learned from her Doctor that nothing had changed in her body.

The baby was born and appeared healthy. He survived, his Mother didn't. Testing revealed the little boy was suffering from mongolism (down's syndrome). Sarah's female kin took care of the infant until they realized he wasn't "normal". The alarm was given to all members of the Negley clan, Sarah's family. They met without Gabby, and decided he couldn't care for the baby, so they started proceedings to institutionalize the baby.

Again, after the paperwork was done toward "putting the child away", another meeting was called but this time Gabby was invited, for they would need his signature on the request. Now they would be free of embarrassment. Child in question would be hospitalized for life and Gabby Shine could leave here through transfer with his job (political move). Mr. Negley saw an end now.

Now called "Big", listened to Mr. Negley spout off how the "boy" (Negley never called him by his proper name, Gabriel) would never make it in social-public activities, get educated, or learn to do simple tasks. Again, he brought up that they had started proceedings to having the "boy" institutionalized.

It didn't take long before "Big" let them know where he stood. Arising from the back of the room where he sat in an old high back chair, he slowly walked to the fireplace area in the "study" and began.

Looking around the room, he became more aggravated.

"Mr. Negley, the "boy" as so indelicately put, has a name. It is Gabriel Fred Shine, named for me and Fred Astaire, Sarah's favorite actor. His pediatrician, Doctor Ashcraft, diagnosed that Sarah's death and Gabriel's malady were brought on due to in my genes I gave each a form of mustard gas poisoning, which apparently; I received in combat. This took Sarah from us and gave our child the autism he now carries. Instead of hiding him or trying to make him live in our world, I shall join him in his world. This will make him happier I'm told. You see, what ya'll don't understand is that his Mother loved him very much. I recall her talking and singing to him while she rocked during her pregnancy. If you think I'm going to lock him up in some hospital or sign some paper that will allow you

14

to institutionalize him, then you got another think coming. This is my son that I'm accountable for. I love him as his Mother did. If you are ashamed of him, then you'll be forbidden to see him." Tears began flowing down his face. "Regardless of how society reacts to him, regardless of how his relations feel about him, regardless of how so-called Christians accept him, I will never, allow nothing and I mean nothing--to hurt him. God gave him to Sarah and me. Granted, I impregnated her with less than perfect sperm.

I'll feel forever that I was responsible for her death and his condition. In her honor and his future, will give me more desire to make his life better and have an unusual quality life. I'll resign my job with the forestry division and open my own business so that I can have my son near me all times. He'll have the best medical and educational care. I'll, seek an extended family, to assist me in his growth. They'll also help me give Gabriel a better sense of security. None of this includes you so don't even try. I just don't understand you people. How could any blood family member consider hiding him under the guise that he doesn't deserve anything? Those of you and your friends that have already determined he'll ever get better, are going to be in for a shock.

The home that Sarah and I bought will be dismantled and the lumber from it will be used to erect a combination business and living area. Most of the home accessories, pipes, electric wiring and furniture will be used also. The lot it stands on will be sold and the money from it will be spent on products for our store. A legacy, will be established and half of the proceeds will be banked for his future."

Sobs could be heard and not just from the ladies but from Mr. Negley as well. During the funeral for Sarah, Negley had shown no emotion, but now, with the embarrassment of what Gabby said to him, caused him to release his tears. In addition, the love Shine showed for his son, broke him down more. "Shine, he said," years from now when I see what kind of young man he's become, I'll see to it he has benefits for the rest of his life." Enraged at the comments made, Shine jumped into Negley's face, grabbed his lapels, and then stormed, "Negley we don't need anything from you, now, or in the future. I'll take out a bond that will state you or anyone from your family cannot ever come near him".

With that he tossed Mr. Negley aside, picked up his fedora and kicked the front door open as he hastened out to take care of his son.

The "bait" shop he built included minnows ("minners" the locals say), various ground worms, a new fishing aid called artificial bait, and the newest in rods and reels. An old fashion cane-pole was fast being replaced. Most of the rod and reels were imported from Sweden and expensive, but as one of the fisherman's wives explained, "a true fisherman doesn't care about the cost, if it will give him an edge, he'll spend his life's savings." The building was strong because he used the wood from his torn-down house and it was made of oak and pine.

He built living quarters connecting to the business. They enjoyed living on the bank of the Tennessee river. "Little Shine" while as a tot, made up for so many of his inadequate abilities by learning to swim like an adult. A large "stage" of slate rock was at the rear of the building where "Little Shine" played. While viewing the great Fred Astaire dancing in so many movies, "Little Shine "admired his dexterity and rhythm and tried to copy this. However, his size seemed to prevent this until the day he discovered chalk.

One glorious day he found discarded math and many other books, including, one on trigonometric functions. Since this related to a circle, it caught his interests. He studied these books but had very little reading skills.

Miss Carolyn Gilbert, local teacher and special caregiver to children with disabilities heard about Gabriel and began spending time with him. Aptitude toward trigonometry that had fascinated many, didn't at first was believed he possessed this "gift". On a spring day, she stopped by to work with him on his reading improvement and met with a child that was "bored" past learning. He yelled at her so loud the "Big Shine" came out of the store to ascertain the problem. Ms. Gilbert jumped up and got his attention by stopping his movements by placing her index finger to her lips that indicated she didn't want him to speak or act.

She picked up a large piece of chalk and handed it to Gabriel. "Now Gabriel, put chalk on floor and draw out what is on your mind", she said. With both adults watching, he began, but first went to his record player and started Fred Astaire singing.

In the next fifteen minutes, with the record playing over and over, he drew out the seeming extravagant exaggeration hyperbola she had ever seen. He then went back to the record player and made a new selection. Once the music began he went back to his drawings on the slate and began dancing, ala Astaire to the formations of the hyperbola. He slid and glided on the slate. The tap dancing shoes he wore so often were making sparks on the terrain and a small crowd gathered to applaud and cheer him on. His father wept. The son smiled. Ms. Gilbert nearly fainted.

As time went by, his friend "Hard Case", visited him often and marveled the way his dancing improved daily. But this was done only to Mr. Astaire's melodious tunes. When "Hard Case" hummed various tunes, "Little Shine" simply stomped instead of dancing

Later in his short life, he made only a few adjustments in his social abilities, but he never forgot Fred Astaire.

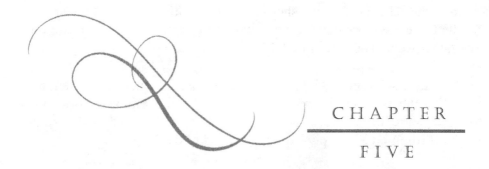

CHAPTER

FIVE

On the way to the court house, the next morning to enlist, he drove slowly and began to reminisce about the men that were enlisting with him. First, it was Doughbelly, the rotund partially bald fellow that was their leader. Full of fun, strong as an ox, and much more intellect than people failed to recognize. He was local but merged with the crew he'd worked with while building the dam as a concrete finisher. Next, other locals, Bones and Monkey. Bones, six feet, one inch, but weighed only one hundred, forty-five pounds. Skinny as anyone around, but quick to learn and devoted to the crew. Monkey, a man for allons. Athletic, smart, stronger than he looked and loved to sail on the river. Rex and Eddie Adams, brothers that didn't fight. Better educated than the others. Plus Pepper, best baseball player in the area. Hoped to go to pros and was saving his money to go for spring training with the St. Louis Cardinals. However, with this war coming, it was doubtful he'd have the opportunity.

Spider, from Louisiana, one hundred percent Cajun. Glad to be here instead of living in the swamps. Had exceptionally long arms and legs. This is how he got his nickname. Little Red, whose age no one knew. Billy Ray had no birth certificate on him. As a matter of fact, no one knew his correct name. Had flaming red hair and came in with Spider. Talented with singing, dancing and musician abilities. Girls just adored him, but he sought to achieve manly pursuits and then he'd meet someone to settle down with and have a lot of red headed babies. It was doubtful he'd be able to join the Navy without proof of birth.

He arrived before the crew came in. Sitting at a window table wearing his best suit with a borrowed briefcase, with their important papers, he began containing himself. He was full of anxiety and worry. Was he doing the right thing? How could he justify this big life change? Would the crew have any money if needed?

At that time, the crew came in, full of laughter and comradeship. This eased his tension and he settled down.

"Well guys, ya'll ready to join up in the great world."
"Yea boy" said Monkey
"Let's drink our coffee first" said Spider.
"Got time for a pool game?" said Rex.
"No, you idiot, this is serious stuff we're about to do" said his brother Eddie.

Doughbelly had found a donut and was chewing it rapidly as he drank his coffee. He didn't have time to talk.
Pepper and Spider had zeroed in on a couple of secretaries that had just arrived and Little Red sat quietly.

They were only a block from the court house which contained the military offices off the Army, Navy, and Marines, so they just walked to a fate unknown to any of them.

They could hear the noise and a man yelling, while coming up the south steps. As they entered the big doors, the man yelling was directing his voice at the men trying to enlist. "Listen you hillbillies and niggers, if you don't keep it quiet out here, none of you will get a chance to get in. So, shut up. By the way you niggers can forget it. We don't need people that can't think or bathe.

With that Billy Ray did the unthinkable, he approached Army Sergeant and Sergeant said, "Sergeant, may I have a word with you?"

"You what?"
"Speak to you."
"About what?"
"About how you talk to us."
"Shut up, idiot."
"Sergeant, I'm going to ask you again to refrain from yelling and

19

cursing these people. I've known most of them most of my life. They are good people. White or colored. They are hard workers and deserve respect

The six feet, four-inch, tall and over two hundred twenty pounds then pushed Billy Ray. After he caught his balance he responded with the most terrific uppercut any one had ever seen. The Sergeants feet went airborne and he hit the floor with a thud, completely unconscious. Billy Ray stepped over him and his men followed. Silence filled the room for a while and then a roar broke out. Men of all color, size, and politically motivation, wanted to shake his hand, pat him on the back or just to tell him how they praised him.

He and his crew kept walking to the sign that indicated the Navy office. They just pushed the door open without knocking and entered. An ensign speaking in a loud voice "What do you guys want?"
Sir we've come to enlist in this here Navy" said Little Red

Calming down, the ensign smiled and said, "Well son you are so young, it appears to me you should join the Boy Scouts first. To the rest of you people, we are not taking enlistments at present. We need billets, instructors and weapons that were lost in the terrible thing that happened at Pearl Harbor. You can wait for a while or join another branch of the military. Understand the Marines, Army, or Coast Guard are taking enlistees."

Billy Ray spoke up and asked, "Where is the Coast Guard office located?"
"In Florence at the post office"
"Can you tell us something about the Coast Guard?" Asked Spider?
"Well, they are a little like the Navy, except they perform near shorelines, don't get involved in aircraft, submarines, nor much hand to hand combat. They don't call the boats or ships those names instead they call them cutters. Need to be in good physical shape to do the tasks given to you. I recommend them."

Thank you, you have given us something to discuss. We appreciate what you do. We will let you know", said Billy Ray.
Outside, the guys talked it over. The Army was DEFINITELY out in joining. Air corp. was a part of the Army and there were no guarantees. So, it was either the Marines or Coast Guard. The discussion was leaning

toward the Marines until they spotted an individual dressed in Navy blue uniform with shined shoes, great haircut and an officer's white cap. He approached them with a smile on his face.

Billy Ray took a chance and asked, "Sir, what branch of the service do you represent"? he asked.

"Sir I'm an officer in the United States Coast Guard" he replied.

"Just the man we need to see. Are you busy this moment?

"As a matter of fact, I am. Doing an investigation on a fractious event that occurred today."

"Well sir, we are considering Joining your service but need to ask questions before we sign up".

"Fellows, will be out in a few minutes. Where may I meet with you?"

"Are you familiar with the City Café here in town?"

"Yes I am. Just go there and wait on me."

"Yes sir, will do".

Lieutenant Greg Fields arrived an hour later, had lunch, and explained what the Coast Guard did. What caught their attention was that they would be paid, fed, clothed, and taught to be offensive and defensive sailors. Attached to the Navy; yet separated. Would leave in two days on a train for New London, Connecticut, where they would be trained. Normally, Camp May, New Jersey would be where they would go, but Lieutenant Fields, was going to sign them up on the new "buddy" plan. This was the site for officer training, so it would be easier to bunch them together.

It was unanimously voted to join the Coast Guard. Billy Ray encouraged the crew to be the best they could be in all endeavors. To practice diligence, good conduct, cleanliness and superior adherence to the Coast Guard.

The next morning. They caught the trolley from Tuscumbia to Florence to be sworn in. Billy Ray had given the Lieutenant the records and Little Red showed up with his own birth certificate and other unnecessary documents. It turned out he was sixteen. His given name was Jake Sellers. Still to his friends he was "Little Red".

In Florence, they not only were sworn in but filled out necessary forms for top secret. Billy Ray was appointed leader of the crew and was given proper vouchers and cash for each person. Upon completion, they returned to Tuscumbia. Billy Ray had to do business and to tell Gloria goodbye. But before they departed from their home, Billy Ray wanted to treat them. After having Dock's hamburgers and R. C. Colas down at Spring Park. Then they went uphill to Davis Department store where he directed the clerk to size up his men and to sack up individual shirts, socks, shoes, pants, belt, underwear, and a jacket. This would be their traveling clothes. He went to the bank and checked out some of his savings, enough for him to purchase his own clothing at New London and traveling clothes from Davis Department store. He instructed his men to check into the Cardiff Hotel for the night. They would leave early in the morning on the New York Special. Now it was time to tell Gloria, and he dreaded it. Rain had started to fall, and as he entered the Palace Drug store to buy toilet articles, he placed his call to Gloria

"Hey Babe" he said on the phone to Gloria at work.

"Wonder if you could meet me at our place after you get off from work?"

"Sure, glad to hear from you. Talked to Bud who told me you were okay."

"Yeah, got a sore noggin but okay." "All right then, see you in about fifteen minutes."

After procrastinating for about ten minutes, he drove to the entrance to Helen Keller's home. Still raining hard as he found their familiar "parking place". Soon she drove in with her green De Soto. Oh! How he dreaded this confrontation, but she was smiling ear to ear anticipating perhaps a proposal. Maybe this would make his job of telling her about joining the Coast Guard easier. She pulled up next to him and he exited and got in on the passenger side. She handed him a hanky for him to wipe the rain from his face. "Hi slugger", as she took the hanky back and kissed him passionately, "Well honey what's going on?" She said.

"I've got some news to tell you and I'm not sure how it's gonna go down with you".

Rain was leaving streaks on the windshield and a slight amount of ice was forming on the hood. The wait for him was just too much for her.

"Well what is it?"

"The boys and I joined the Coast Guard today." Billy Ray blurted out.

"We will be leaving tomorrow morning for training in Connecticut."

She began squealing and beating the dashboard. She turned toward and for the first time in their relationship started slapping him and beating his shoulder. "STOP, GET A HOLD OF YOURSELF" he yelled back at her.

She then began weeping profusely and he just left her alone. Nothing he could do or say seemed to get her out of this terrible mood.

Gloria started shaking her head and exclaimed, "Never fails. people have been running away from me all of my life. First, it was my parents, who left during the great depression after giving me away to her parents. Then my cousin Faye marrying a preacher and moving away to Chattanooga. Some of the teachers I cared so much about just got up and moved away without telling me farewell. AND NOW, you're leaving me after so many promises about our marriage. Believe me, don't ever talk about that again. That too is over. No talk about another job. No talk about having children. No more talk about raising a family. All of that is over. Don't you remember we're orphans, remember we talked about having children and giving them a sense of security. It was so important to me. But no, we must do as Billy Ray wants. My reaction now is this! We are through, I'll find someone that will be with me forever. A good husband and father. That would be good to me and tell me they love me daily. You've not checked on me since Saturday night. Don't remember the last time you told me that you love me.

Silence again as the storm outside was matched by the inside storm. She continued, "I'm sure your next infantile statements will be Oh! Honey, I must do my military obligation.

Or I promise we'll marry when I get some leave. NO BILLY RAY! I've loved you nearly all of my life. The first time I saw you, you were just twelve years old and delivering newspapers vour bicycle. I fell in love with you. Now I'm an adult with wants and needs. Now I see YOUR wants and needs don't include me. Now get out of my car and leave, don't say anything or try to do anything, just leave.

He opened the door and got out but before he closed it he said, "Goodbye Gloria, you're making a mistake. Just try not to make anymore."

He was angered now. She didn't care enough to hear how in fact, he could send for her upon his initial training ended. They could live off base and began their marital relationship.

He got back in his car and followed her for a short distance. It was raining hard now. She looked back in the rear view mirror to get a last glimpse of him, but he was gone. Tears trickled down her face matching the rain flowing down the windshield. On her radio, the melancholy song "Always" was playing.

Next sunrise, the Alabama boys, as they later would be referred as, arrived at the train depot in Tuscumbia, on time, dressed in their new clothing and had a lot of anxiety and excitement. Lieutenant Fields was in full dress uniform. He shook each man's hand and met with Billy Ray inside the depot. There, they discussed details and important directions. Main direction was once they arrived in New York at Grand Central station, they would need to take taxis and go to another station to load on a much smaller train for New London.

The conductor started his colorful shout out with: ALL ABOARD FOR DECATUR, HUNTSVILLE, SCOTTSBORO, CHATTANOOGA, AND POINTS NORTH TO NEW YORK CITY. Billy Ray led his men to the assigned car. Getting them settled was a chore due to the majority of the men had never been on a first-class train. Even explaining about the lavatory was comical. However, they finally settled as the engine started spinning the big steel wheels and the larger iron ones.

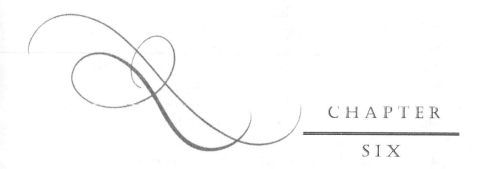

CHAPTER

SIX

In the throes of deep Nazism, the fascistic life of mid-Europe, during the forties of the twentieth century, existed a city infamous as the center of this dreaded "ism", --Munich, Germany.

A very large castle existed for the SS troops as central headquarters. The general in charge was named Renick von Kizziah. He, a veteran of world war one, receiving the Blue Max for heroism. Now, following strong desire to invade America, he formulated the best sabotage plans known to the hierarchy of the war machine. Today he would meet with the stormtroopers that had been selected to participate in the missions.

The building included a room as large as a basketball court with marble floors. As the troops marched in with their hob-nailed shiny boots using the "goose-step" method. General Kizziah beamed. His staff, seemingly happy with the introduction for the troops to their commander; fearfully and full of anxiety, took side-looks to each other knowing that if any of the troops stepped out of line, they would be held accountable.

The General spoke: "To you, the pride of Deutschland, welcome to your new assignments. My part today is to be brief concerning your forthcoming missions. This in a nutshell means, A. You will be highly trained physically. B. You will learn to speak the English language, C. You will learn how to be successful in the efforts of a saboteur. D. You will be rewarded through promotions. E. You will be so greatly trained, you'll be used later as instructors. And finally, F. You will survive and not have to surrender.

Now stand at ease and listen for your name. Major Mueller, the mission director, has previously selected you for a particular -endeavor. Go where he tells you to go. You'll load on trucks and be taken to your initial training site which will begin today. Now the staff is passing you Rhineland wine for our toast." Sergeants assigned to these many missions handed each man a glass of wine. The General spoke again as he lifted his glass. "To our Fuhrer, our Fatherland, our families, we salute and lift our toast in honor." They drank and smiled at their leaders. Little did they know that these men would be sending many of them to their graves.

Among them was Ian von Ingalls, the son of a very rich industrialist who had plants all over the world including one in Ithaca, New York. Young Ian had visited there many times and felt an affection to the American way of life. As a matter of fact, he was educated at Cornell University, where he played American football. His elementary training was something of a paradox. For the first few years of his life, his grandmothers taught him the rudiments of an education. He excelled so much, they took him to a catholic priest who possessed the testing skills of someone so gifted. Ian far exceeded the testing process. The priest along with the grandmothers approached the parents with their findings and suspensions. Their recommendations were to advance him to high school education at once. Family all agreed, but in only two years he'd passed all subjects, but was too young to attend college. Instead the Father, along with Grandfathers, carried him to the adult level of hunting, fishing, hand-to-hand combat, fencing, horsemanship, aviation, and common-sense programs. He especially loved American football and sought those that played the game to teach him the basic mechanics of the game.

Upon mastering the rules and regulations, he persuaded his Father to let him attend Cornell with the promise he'd study Catholicism also. Naturally, he studied classic music, chess, poker and other parlor games.

And now here he was in the Nazi army. This came about when he returned from America for a visit and learned regardless of his father's status, he'd been drafted.

He'd gone through preliminary training, and just one look at him, it would behoove any officer to place him in the Aryan involvement services that Hitler desired so much. He was six feet, three inches, two hundred ten pounds, with blond hair and blue eyes. Muscular, fleet of foot, athlete and exactly what was needed in the sabotage/commando world in that he could speak English without an accent.

His first night in the saboteur section of SS, brought him to the forefront. Tomorrow the men would begin paratroop training followed by hand-to-hand combat positions. Then, weapon expertise, more hand-to hand training, weapon range training with small arms. Explosive ordinance training, swimming, long distance running, speed vehicle driving and ending with learning U-Boat living. Each night they studied American English and first aid. They practiced paratroop training often.

Their finals would be a paratroop jump, fully packed and in bad weather conditions. Over Algeria, was where they would make the fateful venture. Should they survive, the next day they would leave on an airplane for Costa Rica where they would jump again. Once they arrived on the designated islands, they would separate in squads and board the U-Boats (submarines) for the shores of the southern half of the United states. Exactly where wasn't told at this point but it would be a point so compelling, that teamwork would be the first order of business.

The last night in Germany was spent abbreviating themselves and preparing for the mission. Even though they had rucksacks, pistols with ammo, dagger, food, water, camping supplies, first aid packets, they knew they must adjust for the jump. In the JU fifty-two, they left one of their training sites in Malta and proceeded to jump just over Constantine near the sea, in Algeria. It was a cold night with snow flurries and they were jumping too close to the ground. Ian was number ten in the jumps, and as soon as the green light came on, he buckled tight for the fall. As he exited the plane, a swift sheer hit him driving him under the rear wheel and knocking the wind out of him and partially unconscious. In a split- second he quit in the spiral and locked his knees and ankles together to make a straight fall. This worked and able to measure his distance to the surface. Hitting in a swaying motion, he adjusted to rolling his back on the ground and to expect the drift and drag.

27

Unfortunately, his neck was forced into a bridge position and it made him to black out.

When he came to, the snow was falling harder and the sleet seemed to be colder. He laid on the ground for a while trying to be aware of his environment. Took only a few seconds of; "eye-batting" before he tried to move his body. Dizziness was still there but he was confident he wasn't hurt. Finally, he moved. Sitting up, he began looking all around and picked up the horizon. Dragging his feet under him gave confidence and he stood. Still with his eye on the horizon, he pulled his pocket compass out and began to get his bearing. First thing he did was to collapse the chute and pull it toward him. Next was to find rucksack and locate his flashlight. Standing very erect with new found battery-powered "torch" in his hand, he flashed the beam of light all around the terrain he'd landed in. It seemed to be bowl shaped about thirty meters in width and about forty meters in length. While scanning the area he located an abandoned cave, just large enough for him to get out of the weather elements. The scan also revealed lumps of coal that he could use to keep warm. Situation told him not to attempt to connect with his group. The bump, drag and sudden stop had "blacked" him out for a while and still nursing a concussion he'd received playing American football at Cornell University, he knew he'd been pion another. He had a terrific headache that prevented him from seeing very good. He also was very hungry and tired.

Gathering up his chute and rucksack, he made his way toward the cave using his beam to guide him. Once there, he cleaned out the cave and saved the wood that was inside for fuel. Inside he placed his chute so that it could serve as his bed. Rucksack was placed there also. Returning to where he thought he saw the lumps of coal, he gathered up the heavy solid lumps and returned to the hole. One of the lumps was a rock but the others was coal-lumps. Building a fire with scraps of kindling wood, paper and coal, he returned to the field and loaded up with more coal. Along the way, he found more rocks and gathered them also. Surrounding the fire with the rocks, he hoped they would absorb heat and keep him warm throughout the night.

In his rucksack was a medium can of beef stew and a carton of saltine crackers. His canteen was full of water and his alternative contained schnapps. A meal much needed he thought! Upon completion of the tasty morsels, sleep grabbed him. He'd already taken a couple of aspirin and the headache was trying to subside. Placing his weapon on the side of his face and away from the fire, he placed the safety latch on.

At sunrise, he awoke to the knowledge that the fire had gone out and he had a chill. Standing up, he retrieved his pistol and inserted it into his holster. Packing the rucksack was no problem. Even refolded the chute and placed it back into its bag.

He walked north from the cave until he came to the macadam road where trucks were speeding east and west. Placing his helmet on his head, he began trying to find his comrades by walking east. After about a mile, he came up on a cobblestone bridge and took a break. As he opened his rucksack to pull out a chocolate bar, the Holy Bible took a tumble to the surface. Picking it up and dusting it off, he turned to Psalm 91:11 that said, FOR HE SHALL GIVE HIS ANGELS CHARGE OVER YOU....TO KEEP YOU IN ALL WAYS...then THEY SHALL BEAR YOU UP IN THEIR HANDS, LEAST YOU DASH YOUR FOOT AGAINST A STONE.

Walking again for another hundred yards or so, he came to a crossroads that would change his life. Should he turn to his left, he would find ships and other transportation that could give him freedom if he hid correctly. Turning back, he would be walking westerly and should find Algerians that would be glad to hide him. This would guarantee them cash money. Much needed and appreciated.

Should he continue easterly, he would be in the bay and the ripples of the waves would generate subluxation and possibly drown. So, the alternative would be to turn right and go south to the city. He'd only gone about a mile when he saw a two-ton truck headed his way. As it got closer, he deemed that the soldiers standing up on the back of the truck and shouting, were German. As it got closer, he realized that the men were members of his organization and were shouting his name. He couldn't help but smile when he heard one to say, "where have you been—you slacker--."

CHAPTER

SEVEN

Colonel William "Wild Bill" Donovan, arrived at the anteroom near the office of the President of the United States of America, Franklin Delano Roosevelt, on time. He'd been summoned to meet with his old friend, whom he knew from Columbia Law School and when the President was the Assistant Secretary of the Navy.

Mr. Cordell Hull, the Secretary of State in nineteen forty- two, had summoned him to meet with President when the Yalta Conference ended. This was a complete mystery to the Colonel. Why did President Roosevelt want to see him? He was an officer in the U, S. Army, so anything with the Navy wasn't in anyway a part of his expertise. But, the President was successful in filling him with anxiety at the same time he was following orders.

The appointment secretary brought him a cup of coffee, hoping it would somehow calm him down. Pacing back and forth had -rattled" her and she needed him to be more patient. In her job, she had noticed that people that were about to enter through the hallowed doors to meet with the most important -man in the world, were literally shaken when their names were called. Colonel Donovan appeared calmer than most, but the pacing gave him away, he had anxiety.

Time was 1500 hours, weather was great for a spring day. No rain nor windy. However, the importance of this meeting required a lot of impute from whomever would be attending today. Calm down! Calm down! He kept telling himself. Finally, he sat his coffee down and took a seat. Thinking of his days in law school where he learned about the word —constant—in the proper forms of adjective and noun. In formulating any type of sentence involving a meeting with the President of the United States, he hoped the results would be adjectives and as his friends in the iron and steel business would say, "long-bearing".

At 1530 hours, he was asked to enter and meet with the President. Expecting a big grin, jovial greeting and polite initial conversation; all just didn't happen. Instead the look was stern, proper posture in his chair, smoking a cigarette, and coat removed, gave the Colonel the feeling that something tragic like the bombing of the Japanese over Hawaii, had happened again. Lord, I hope not I He said to himself. He was motioned to sit at a Queen Anne blue chair.

"Hello Bill, how are you and your family?"
"Doing all right sir."
"Guess you wonder why I sent for you huh?"
"Indeed, I do sir"
"Well it's this way."
He then moved his chair back, adjusted his position to be more comfortable and pushed a button on his beautiful desk. No clutter nor stack of papers hid the button. It was plain for all to see. Taking this moment, Bill looked around trying to see if anyone else occupied the area. There was none, but in a short time, Mr. Cordell Hull, Secretary of State and Mr. Henry Stinson, Secretary of War; entered through a small door that seemed to be hidden. Colonel Donovan stood. Alas! He thought, these are the two guys that signed off for promotions for the military. "Was he being promoted, is this the reason I'm here. Where was his family? They attended promotion ceremonies."

Both men being formal came over to him, shook his hand, and then led him over to a den type setting that included a large 'coffee" table and two over-sized sofas. The President was Pushed over by apparently a secret service man that stealthy entered, moved the President and left the room.

The President spoke first:

"Colonel Donovan, reason you're here today is due to some events happening and more to happen. They include the Nazi invading the shores of our great country, and we've determined you are the man to stop them and save us all. Your expertise and your knowledge of European culture will be to our benefit. We want you to establish groups of experienced and trusted friends In Europe and then through our military bring in those you trust that can be taught how to stop saboteurs. In Europe, as you know, knowledge and communication have been shut down to us. Open it back up. Use the intelligence to establish war plans. Use the intelligence what we must do to protect our country. Today you are a Colonel in the Army. Tomorrow you will be In charge with the rank and pay of a brigadier general. This is a "type" of cabinet war detachment. It has been named as the acronym: O.S.S., but the proper name is: Office of Strategic Services. You will be director of all operations. Bill Stephenson from the United Kingdom recommended you. Likewise, he recommended Brigadier General John Mac Gruder of the U. K. to be your director of foreign intelligence, and report to you. It is important you find someone of this type for Far East Intelligence.

Your office will be the U.S. S. Potomac. A Navy Commander is awaiting in the anteroom when you are released here, will take you to your quarters. In addition, a small sport boat is attached and when you are ready to begin flights; he will take you to a private airstrip.

Now, all of that said, let's begin your duties and missions. Assemble your staff and instructors. The Commander will be your administrative assistant and comes highly recommended by the Department of Navy." President Roosevelt picked up a few pages of contracts and read to himself. "His name is James Wright, from Petersburg, Tennessee." The President replied.
Continuing about the dangers facing them, the President added. "We were sabotaged at Pearl Harbor, Mexico, and the Indian wars. If you remember your History."

'Yes sir, I do."

"Well this is what I want. This is what America wants. Generals and Admirals recommend the same Let us stop sabotage."

"Agree"

"To be blunt, get it done."

"Directives sir?"

"Read all files the Commander will give you. These are given to you by the men present. They've accumulated a great deal of intelligence but now I need them for more activities. Just General Donovan and yours truly from now on."

"Understand sir. As soon as I read the files and formulate plans I'll be in touch."

"That's what I want General. Now let us dismiss. Thank you so much."

With that the doors opened; and the room emptied. The secret service man approaching the President, stopped and handed a business card to Donovan. He glanced at it but didn't study. The Secretaries seemed to disappear back in the walls of the office. Donovan went out the anteroom door, then remembered his manners and turned to shake the President's hand, but he also had disappeared. Later he was told the handshakes weren't needed from department heads and now he was one. Walking out the white house, he pulled the card and read 'U6418 Y"27"

CHAPTER

EIGHT

At the Tuscumbia, Alabama, train station. The Alabama boys (as they would be later known); arrived from a hay truck driven by mutual friend.

They were escorted by the conductor, Mr. Wayne Clark, to their Pullman car. Mr. Clark had already collected the vouchers from Billy Ray Coleman, so therefore it was permissible to have a seat.

Meanwhile, Billy Ray stood on the back steps of the caboose hoping to get a glance of Gloria should she show up. She didn't so he reentered and made his way to the Pullman that contained his men. He'd been placed as officer-in-charge and would interpret orders and direct them on how to react to social movements and who, what, where, and how they were to be representing the Coast Guard.

Allowing them to settle down and sleeping again, was a good move. This gave Billy Ray a few moments to attempt to get over the fact she hadn't come by to wish him farewell. Going back through the many years together brought him to the edge of grief and sorrow. Tears did run down his cheeks as he turned to look out the window and not be seen by his friends.

All were asleep except Doughbelly, who was reading "Captain Marvel" comic book for the umpteenth time. He felt so much sympathy for Billy Ray, that he began disliking Gloria who heaped this on Billy Ray, that didn't deserve this.

Billy Ray pulled out the orders and re-read them. They would stay on the "Chattanooga Choo-Choo" until they arrived in New York at Grand Central. There they would transfer to a smaller line that was ear-marked to take troops to the Coast Guard Academy, arriving tomorrow afternoon. Finally caught some sleep and was awaken mid-day for lunch. He alerted the guys and explained where and how they were to act. Especially, table manners. He then directed them to go to the "head" to clean-up.

In the latter part of the day, they arrived at appointed place. Exiting the Pullman, they all entered the main rotunda and were amazed at the kiosk assembled and strolled on through to he main doors and stepped out on the sidewalks to experience.

New York. The noise, smells, hustle-bustle, traffic, and so much more; excited them to no end. With mouths agape, a thousand questions and assurance gone by, the Alabama boys soon turned to Billy Ray for some leadership. "Fellas, there is so much for all of us to learn. Now let's go inside and get something to eat. I'm buying."

They entered and were taking back at the ingredients used in preparing food. Oriental foods with burnt chicken. Scandinavian meals made with sheep and some other type of animal. Russian with the largest red beets they had ever seen. Jewish specialties with use of eggs unlike anything they had ever seen. They took seats at a large round table and just sat staring at each other.

Doughbelly, the astute lover of food, noticed a table loaded with a large family and eating a round food pie by the slice. The family was enjoying the food tremendously and Doughbelly knew at that moment he must have some of it. "Billy Ray, reckon what they call them slices of good smelling chow?"
"Don't know Doughbelly, why don't you go over there and ask?'

He did, and after the Father's laughter, he presented Doughbelly with a small slice of a unit called "Pizza", which he consumed with the gusto of an Alabama blue tick hound. Explaining to the Alabama boys as well as Billy Ray about the food and the exotic flavor, Doughbelly requested that they buy this at once and spread it around. Eddie was dispatched by Billy Ray to order three large

Supremes and accompanying coca- colas. Eddie got the cash to pay and Spider, Pepper, and Monkey, picked the orders up. Doughbelly was the first to begin eating. Not a crumb was spared and the Italian family that had taught them what a "pizza pie" was, marveled at the consumption.

Again, they walked outside for some fresh air and to live as the inhabitants did used a small amount of their advance pay to buy souvenirs. Mostly they bought the one-dollar wristwatches from street vendors. Within an hour, they caught the trolley provided for them to ride to the smaller train station located on a spur track.

Once aboard the train destined for New London, Connecticut, they settled down with bellies full of Pizza, and sacks of Candy and a new item called potato chips. The trip was uneventful except for a group of men from Ohio, who called the Alabama boys "Hillbillies." This resulted in Little Red slugging one, who didn't wake up for a while.

The guys sat around in-route to their training center talking about the events since they left home. So much had already been done and learned. They hadn't gotten use to the new clothing Billy Ray had bought for them, nor the cash he'd given to them to exist on. A new wristwatch. Great tasting food. Ice cream and cherries. Smiling women who enjoyed making eye-contact. For some reason, they preferred the little guy with red hair it was no secret, to the others, Red's smile could capture any woman.

The years of working and living together brought them to the throes of perfect teamwork. Like any set of brothers, it was this way: we can fight each other, but no one can come in and jump one of their own. Must share at times. Nurse when others are sick. No jealousy between each other. But the number one credo was simply, love, protect and abide with Billy Ray Coleman, their all-time champion and hero.

The train, on time, came in the New London area. Puffing ebony smoke, white steam billowing out, the one car train began to brake and was timed to be exact with the deck connected to the new station here. Once completely stopped, all troops dismounted. The Alabama boys were first with their bag and baggage. Waiting were two N. C. 0.'s who began barking orders directing them to a bus. Once aboard, they placed what they owned in their laps.

Billy Ray's name, was called and he was directed to get on a grey-covered Jeep, that would take him to the officer's billets at the Academy. He looked back at his men on the bus and took a large gulp. Back home they would identify this as he'd "spoiled" them by taking care of all their needs even back to the days as "concrete finishers" while they aided in building Wilson Dam on the majestic Tennessee river.

It was almost like a Mother taking care of her children on their first day of school. He turned away for a second and then looked forward, did a silent prayer and immediately received the impression that all of them were in God's hands. Even if they were grown men, HE would take care of them now. Today they began a new life.

CHAPTER

NINE

Arriving at the Naval yard, General Donovan and Commander Wright, exited the large black Hudson and rapidly made their moves in entering the U. S. Potomac.

Wright and the administration leader named Carolyn Claudia, led him to his living quarters and the main office. His private office was somewhat hidden; and the eating area was extremely large and roomy. This room was designed for the President and his wheelchair. He loved to be in the kitchen and on occasion cooked some. For now, it was a meeting room. The other staff were headquartered at the front of the craft.

General Donovan pulled fifty dollars from his front pocket and asked Ms. Carolyn to send someone to the PX and purchase food, drink and especially steaks. On board was a charcoal burner to cook the steaks. The General, taking the files from Commander Wright and Ms. Carolyn, went below to his office to study and formulate plans.

That night, he came topside to eat an evening meal. The kitchen was closed but he made himself a sandwich and soup anyway. He was hungry also needed strength from food. He would probably work through most of the evening he thought.

The next morning, after breakfast that had been prepared for staff and the General, Wright got in the car with a designated navy driver that was directed to take the General to shops that carried civilian clothing that would be appropriate and would fit him. He would not be his regular driver though, only the General had the right to select people he would be working with.

General Donovan, who; lived in the Washington area; with his wife Ruth Ramsey Donovan and his family. Though madly in love with all of them he knew he must center his activities for the military first and family second. Many the time he laughed at those stances. Being a devout Catholic who attended morning mass as often as he could and the fact that he once studied at the seminary for the priesthood, it was a natural that Christ came first, then Country, followed by family.

After going shopping, he directed the driver to return to the ship. Driver, was excused and Bill took the car and went to see his family. Embracing and kissing each other went on for a while. Ruth had missed him so much and just couldn't let him go. This is a mistake he told himself, it's going to be so hard leaving again, but to keep them out of harm's way he must separate living with them. However, he spent the remainder of the day with his love ones. Walked into the kitchen as she was preparing dinner, with her back to him. She wore a lime green sweater with a gray skirt. To him she looked wonderful. He approached her and circled her waist with his arms and bent over and kissed her on the neck. She dropped the potatoes she was peeling, turned, looked direct into his eyes and smiled. He touched her cheek and then kissed her again. She pressed herself to him and purred like a kitten.

Indeed, it was hard to leave so he spent the night there and took off at sunrise. He and his wife needed each other so much. It simply not their nature to seek love from other people Just each other. She was weeping when he went out the door.

That day was spent with Commander Wright going over present and future applications for those needed to work with the OSS He approved those presently on staff on board except for one, Sergeant Major Timothy Talbot. Main problem here was obviously he loved to drink any kind of alcohol. Too much intelligence passing through so many people to risk a drunk talking too much. But, his file revealed what a strong warrior he was and would be a great body-guard/driver for the General. Only way to solve this matter would be a one-on-one interview for correct decision.

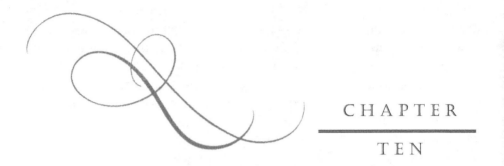

CHAPTER

TEN

"Sir, Sergeant Major Tim Talbot reporting as ordered" "At ease Top, take a seat"

"Reason I called you in was because of your record. I am privy to bust you to a private due to your love of the bottle. Too many DWI, public intoxication and brawls. My God man you must have dirt on your former commanders to get away with so much. Have you ever been dried out?"

'No sir. No one, has ever talked to me the way you just did"

"Don't know why. You're a dud. Even with a college degree, you lack intelligence. Even with your excellent combat experience, you lack the proper way to conduct yourself. No, just no way. This Army doesn't need someone like you to serve in any leadership capacity. You were sent here to get out of somebodies- hair, apparently. Is that not correct Sergeant?"

"Thought I was sent here to work for you in S3 activities. After all, I do have a top-secret clearance. If you perceive I need to make adjustment, such as my drinking, consider it done. Give me another chance and I won't let you down sir."

"I don't know why I should do that"

"Army is my only way of life. My wife and children left me when I was sent to North Africa due to her feelings for another man. Drinking started then but will stop It. Again, I won't let you down. Just give me a job, please."

"Step outside Sergeant Major, while I muse over this."

"Yes sir"

He pushed a button to Carolyn's desk. "Yes sir, General, what can I do for you?"

"Do you know where Commander Wright is located?" "In his office sir. Do you want me to fetch him?" "Yes, -send him down please."

"Need me General?"

"Yes, need to talk to you about the Sergeant Major." 'What about him?"

"Your opinion."

"Obviously, he is a top soldier. Has a drinking problem, but just needs to be given care. He can overcome I'm sure. If memory serves, his wife divorced him, throwing him into a pit. Now we are at war, I expect him to adjust correctly."

"What job would you give him?"

"One that keeps him busy, with responsibility, and be in a posture to be scrutinize daily."

"Well, I think you've given me an idea. I'll make him my driver and bodyguard. What do you think?"

"Perfect sir, just perfect."

"Tell Carolyn to send him in."

He entered in the proper military manner and saluted.

"Top, know what I'm going to do. From this point on, you'll have a dual job. I'll keep you, no busting. You're my driver and personal bodyguard. Leave here today, get new uniforms and civilian suits. Carolyn will give you the money to cover your costs. By the way, buy new civilian shoes. Go by arms and check out two pistols, ammo, and body holsters. Wouldn't hurt to have military belt, holster and a .45 also. Get necessary haircut, toilet articles, towels etc. You'll sleep here also. Then report back to me for inspection."

The two men helped each other throughout the war. The Sergeant Major, never drank again and on so many times he risked his life to save the General.

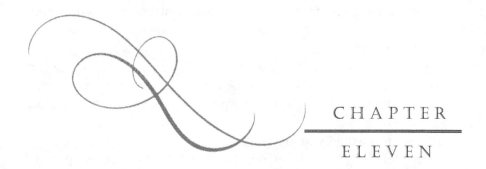

CHAPTER

ELEVEN

He completed his calls at the detachment, went back to Tuscumbia for setting up bank services, ate lunch and picked up new clothes from Davis Department store and headed back to Pride's Landing. He drove around to the back door, picked up the many gifts he'd picked up for Heidi and Sissy and knocked on the door. Sissy let him in and announced that Heidi hadn't left from work coming home yet. Probably would be in another hour.

He went into the extra bedroom and hung his clothes up. He knew he couldn't stay here over two nights and would travel to Courtland, about eighteen miles, on Monday. While waiting for Heidi, he bathed and changed clothes. Soon, Sissy came in the kitchen and made a pot of coffee. Her next few moments of remarks she made opened his eyes as to events that had occurred lately. What she told him was that many available and married men had been making advances at Heidi. Due to her being a German matron, not all were happy with her being free. Threats had been made, so Sissy obtained some weapons, placed extra locks on doors and windows, and placed "Lucy", Billy Ray's Jack Russell dog, outside on alert

Heidi just didn't walk into a room ladylike, but rather entered the room as someone who planned on taking it over. She slammed the front door and yelled out "Sissy" with a smile in her voice. She made the turn to the kitchen and froze. Her smile faded when she saw Billy Ray. Her faced glowed... The locking of their eyes produced enough energy and immediate powerful love unlike any either had ever experienced. "You're beautiful Billy Ray Coleman" she said with a melting voice. He was totally stunned. He said nothing but took long strides toward her, folded his arms around her and then kissed her. Sissy walked out the back door to see his car and to leave them alone.

They too went outside as Sissy was marveling over his car. Heidi looked at it briefly, but her attention was on him. He took her hand and the two strolled off toward the boat-dock. Lucy trotted behind them. The next day, Sunday, Sissy packed them a picnic basket for them as the sail was raised on his old skiff and they sailed off toward the middle of the Tennessee River, and just let all of God's nature take over. Late that afternoon they took the 1940 Blue Convertible to Iuka, Mississippi, where they wed.

'SUE', real name Hedwig Coen, beautiful Jewish lady, was blackmailed to accompany George Amis, a German spy to Florence, Alabama, to appear as his wife. Her understanding was all o her family would not be a part of the holocaust if she did this. Of course, this didn't happen, all were gassed in the "showers" at Dacha.

She played her part, as Amis' wife, and was temporarily freed, but was still under house arrest, and lived in the home of Sissy Goodloe at "Pride's Landing". This was done by the only man she'd ever wanted as a friend, lover and possible husband, Billy Ray Coleman. He was still in the Coast Guard, but she had not seen him for a long time. He telephoned "Sissy" inquiring about her, and occasional message was given. Not that she understood everything, after all Southern English was hard to comprehend, but the intent was there and that was all she needed. In her heart, she felt she'd never see her Germany again, but then, as a Jew, she knew she'd never find a "real" home in Europe again but here, in a country she'd learn to love, a future could be possible. Hardest part was learning the language, but she took any opportunity to do this. The radio words are what she learned the most. From the ladies at work who started to give her insight into the meanings.

Sissy taught her how to dress, how to make favorable impressions, and how to slowly become Americanized. She learned to drive an automobile and obtained the required license. The grocery store where she worked afforded her the knowledge needed for cooking these delightful southern dishes. Quickly, she learned and how to make, the famous southern ice tea. Bar B Q meats were her favorite. Roasted corn on the cob was a true delicacy. Water cooled watermelon American version of biscuits, banana pudding, fried chicken and even cornbread, were part of her daily diets that were made at the hands of the lovely Sissy. Gradually, she learned to cook all of these great meals plus she was already a gourmet in preparing venison and wild turkey, therefore as the local people would say, "you are going to make someone a great wife" Oh! I hope so, she'd reply. Little did they know she already had someone in mind.

One night as she and Sissy did their daily rituals of make-up trials the phone did ring, and her heart jumped into her throat. Oh, please let it be Billy Ray, I want to hear his voice so bad. And it was. She had to wait though until Sissy talked to him. They were like Mother and son, and the subjects they talked about baffled her. At last she got her opportunity and said:

"HI Billy Ray, I miss you"

"Well glad to hear that because I've been thinking about you"

"Oh really"

"Yes, and by the way your speaking English is better"

"Thank you. I try hard, because I want for you to understand"

"I'll be seeing you soon. Got a big surprise for you"

"What Billy Ray? Are you going to marry me?

Laughingly he answered, "Slow down, nothing has been said about marriage. Just got a special gift for you, we call it a surprise, means something you are getting' and you were not expecting it"

"Guess I should say Okay. Huh?"

Billy Ray still laughing primary at her attempt to be subtle, but her German-Jewish manner of straight forwardness over took her training to become a "southern belle". He replied "Heidi, there are many things we will talk about when I'll see again. Just keep on doing what you've been working to learn about in changing your life and we'll take our relationship to a higher level. Do you understand what I'm talking about?"

"Not really, Billy Ray Coleman, but when I see you again could you kiss me. I'd like that."

"Sure, we can do that, I'm a gentleman but not crazy." "I do not understand"

"Then yes, I'll kiss you"

Days turned into weeks and Heidi looked toward the west hoping for a glimpse of Billy Ray walking up the road for Pride's Landing. Even though no time date had been set, she knew he'd appear without letting them know first. She surmised that he would do things mysteriously, and she'd better get prepared for it. She wanted him for her husband. Having him as the father of her children would be exactly how she wanted her life to work out. She would convert her German ways and become an American. There were Jewish people in this area and she talked with them in Hebrew when the opportunity arose, but if Billy Ray wanted her to become more gentile and less Jewish, she would. "This, is love," she thought. How it would be in the future all depended on what Billy Ray wanted.

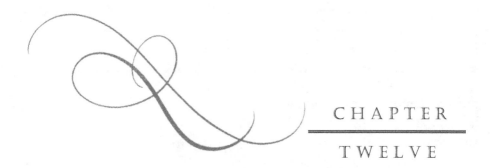

CHAPTER
TWELVE

"What is going on?" exclaimed Pepper,

"I've run so much lately, my holes in my socks have new blisters growing out of them."

"My arms are so sore from push ups that I can't lift them up to comb my hair "said Bones.

"Wonder why this excess training is being pushed on us just as we are preparing to leave?" Said Spider.

"Beats me but I can handle that part, but the extra time on the rifle range is doing a number on my ears" said Little Red.

"Yeah" they all said at once.

"Chief, how are the Alabama boys doing with the extra training" asked Captain Moody?

(Pause)

"Tired "said Chief Petty Officer Gaskins. Both laughed.

"Guess you're trying to figure all of this out"

"Did cross my mind" "Top secret."

"Oh, I see. What's next for them and how may I serve you and them."

"Waiting on Washington. Just keep them busy. Hold off a bit on the P. T., work on Coast Guard cutter movements until they receive their orders. I don't know anything else at this point.

"Aye-Aye Sir"

He left the command office and after exiting the front door, did a lot of head scratching.

WASHINGTON D. C.

"Ensign Hall, I want you to take these orders and files to

the Commanding Officer, U. S. Coast Guard Academy. Make sure only he gets these papers. Wear class "A" uniform and take the de Havilland. Call the pilot now and have the plane prepared."

"Ms. Carolyn, send in the papers I have assorted on your desk about the Poconos."

She did and stood by for directions from the General. He just ignored her and went back to the memorandum he was writing.
NEXT DAY

"Ms. Carolyn, please come in and bring your pad." asked General Donovan.

As directed she knocked and entered. "Yes sir"

"Need for you to connect me with the Department of Defense, U. S. Marine Division, administration General and uh get me his name, file etc. first. Okay?"

"Yes sir", took an about - face and exited to do the request from the General.

After an hour, information requested arrived. His name was General Tom Thompson, from North Carolina, graduate of the Naval academy. Bronze star recipient and combat hero from world war One. Highly rated in his present job. After reading his file over and noted that he did possess a top- secret clearance as well as s-3 director for the corp.

"U. S. Marines, General Thompson speaking sir' into the phone.

"General, this is General Donovan, Army. It is very important I speak to you alone today if possible in a private location"

"About what"

"Can't tell you on the phone. But if it is an imposition to meet with you at your place, perhaps you could meet me at mine. I can send a car for you in an hour and we'll conduct our business."

"Let me ask you General Donovan, who is your boss?" "Only, the President of the United States!'
Pause

"Send your car sir."

In about a couple of hours, General Thompson arrived in his "greens" with full metals. Crisp sort of a man and all military, Donovan thought. He'd have to be mellowed.

"Well, what could I do for you General Donovan?

"Thompson, it's this way: I run the O.S.S., you've heard of us, right?"

"Indeed"

"I want trained China Marines, commandos or whatever you have to assist me in training other branches of the services to form commando groups that can shut down and capture saboteurs we feel are about to invade our shores. I've reviewed your files and am absolute you will be greater serving our country, in addition to the corps, as adjacent duties working for me in the O.S.S. I'll be calling on you frequently for assistance. Do you have any questions?"

"Yes sir, I do? What about my superiors?"

"General Thompson, have them contact me or the President, but I assure you, I'm your only superior now. Now leave here, go back to your office and start pulling records and issuing orders to send me at least ten men, with Gunnery, O.I.C., three officers and five enlisted men to go to the new training facilities I'm having built in the Poconos. First things first, Get the O.I.C. and the Gunnery in touch with me a.s.a.p. Cut the orders sending them to the marine barracks in Lejeune. We'll re-cut once facilities are completely. Remember, men requested must possess top-secret clearance ratings. You are to have private meeting with them and give brief plus swearing them in as members of the O.S.S. Once this is done, contact my assistant, Ms. Carolyn and tell her the men are sent to Lejeune. I'll get in touch with you and them then.

NEW LONDON

Graduation day: First, Billy Ray crossed the stage, number one in the class. Received his credentials and commission, saluted Chief Gaskins and gave him a dollar.* While receiving his scrolls, Captain Moody whispered to him to go to headquarters office and wait on him.

Next, the Alabama boys graduated, receiving cheers and applause from the other graduates for the excellent job they did. When they returned to their seats a message was taped to their seats that said: Meet Captain Moody and Chief Gaskins at 1700 hours in the Quad. They thought; any celebration, any break, orders given; what?

Immediately, Billy Ray made his way to headquarters and entered the office to wait on the commander. The Alabama boys marched to the quad with Doughbelly leading them. Shortly, Chief Gaskins arrived and put the guys at ease. They must wait on their Captain. Anxiety was evident in each man due to the unknown. They didn't nor had ever experienced anxiety without Billy Ray there to sooth matters over.

Captain Moody entered his office with a smile on his face. "Again,

congratulations on your commission"
Standing at attention, Billy Ray said "Again, thank you sir."

Moody just nodded and went to the back room for a while and upon returning, brought with him a stack of papers and placed them on his desk.

"Got your orders here." Silence

When you and your guys joined the Coast guard, you filled out many forms. One of them was an application for top-secret clearance. It was granted to you and your men. Now you are being assigned to train as a commando with the O.S.S. Your men are going with you and we'll explain this in a minute, but first, let me explain more in detail. At this will be a big day for you when I tell you that upon completion of the commando training, you and your men will be sent back to your home area, to capture the perpetrators who will attempt to explode the dam and nearby nitro plant."

Again - silence

He started up again.
The course will be manned by Marines, "China"marines to be exact and they will train you on how to be defensive and offensive in hand-to-hand combat. It will take about two and a half weeks to complete. Additional training that will give you the upper hand in surviving combat situations. Too intricate now to explain because we are studying the curriculum well be presenting. I'll need your help when we give this information to your men. They'll ask a lot of questions about details which don't have the answers yet. General Donovan will educate you and the men later. But, in the meanwhile, let them know they'll get extra money, and will travel a bit more. Training will be more severe there than it is here. Let me tell you one thing I do know for sure. When you go home, you'll be required to remain in hiding and incognito. I'm told someone you know back home will be in assistance. Don't know who yet, but before you leave the area you will know

."

Later, they met at the quad in a closed group outside meeting. The Alabama boys were less than happy to undergo more "infantry" type training, but the trust they have in Billy Ray superseded the initial discomfort of the assignment.

General Donovan's staff of excellent people, had a group that knew how to assemble sites, equipment, and personnel to activate training for most of the needs to get the job done. They selected the Poconos resort area for this type of training. It contained the ingredients to get the job done. Some facility work needed to be done, so the Army Corp of Engineers was dispatched to proper areas to complete the tasks.
China Marines, a mixture of "lifers" and naval academy grads, were originally a part of the 4th Regiment that were stationed in Shanghai from 1927-1941. Assigned there to protect American citizens and American properties, during Chinese revolution and the second Sino-Japanese war.

CAMP LEJEUNE, N. C........
The assembled staff "China" Marines, destined for the Poconos met with Generals Donovan and Thompson at the gym that was closed tight and highly guarded with the best security on the base.

"Men, we're about to send you to the Pocono resort to serve as Cadre in a training unit for commandos. We are about to be attacked by saboteurs who will try to explode a lot of key establishments all over the mainland of the United States. Plans are drawn up and you are to follow them in detail. Study the training plans and execute them when the first group of personnel arrive in about a week. I wish to send you there in the morning, so you can get familiar with the terrain. Teach them well. Should you have any problems, contact General Thompson. Now who is the ranking officer here?"

"That would be me sir. My name is Major William Cameron Please let me introduce you to my assistants, Captain J. J. Fairer, and the NCOIC is Gunnery Milton McWroten. We'll do the job sir, did a little of this in China."

'Good- -Good - leave in the morning. Paper work and orders plus the plans are in these bags."
The bags were given out. The Generals departed. Pocono staff departed the next morning. Graduates of the Coast Guard were set to leave in three days. Captain Moody would handle them. Meanwhile, while waiting to catch transportation, the Alabama boys continued training on a cutter.

CHAPTER

THIRTEEN

Back in Alabama, seemingly, all was the same. But, Bud Goodloe knew better. He'd been contacted by the newly formed O.S.S. and had been included in an event that was greatly disturbing him. The Nazi was about to attack the home of his birth. From what he understood, they were planning on exploding Wilson dam and the nitrogen plant that was one hundred yards or more away, that would result in the banks to be dissolved, dam destroyed, no utilities, and mass murder. Not to mention flooding. He'd been recently called back to service in the Marine Corp and was being assigned with the state adjunct general office as ranking Colonel. Now he was to gather five plywood fishing boats with outboard motors, gallons of gas, take Billy Ray's boat and have it refurbished, eight pistols with proper amount of ammunition; rations for nine men for at least a week, scout out an island for camping; plus, camping gear, fishing gear for all the men, and individual used rifles with ammo.

For safety reasons, the Bait Shop on the Lauderdale side would need to be moved and the business shut down. But how was he to do that without telling the owner why and breach security. Keeping all of this would be hard and all he had to work with him was Captain Billy Norman, who normally worked at the utility department in unison with Tennessee Valley Authority, the great supplier of electricity for the mid-south. He'd been drafted via Army reserves to return to active duty and would soon be sent to Fort Benning, Georgia for advance training. But recently, Washington sent orders for him to report to Colonel Bud Goodloe for special assignment. What? The two men took a boat excursion to the island near the dam. Satisfied this location would be what the needs called for, they banked and went in Bud's car to the U.S. Marshall's office in the Lauderdale court house. Something had to be done about Big Shine's bait shop.

Marshall Wayne Davis was glad to see Bud. They had been childhood friends and had been estranged from each other, as well as other classmates for a long time.

"Hey Bud, long time no see" the Marshall said, as he pumped Bud's hand.

"What can I do for you or is this just a social call."

Bud explained:

"Wayne you do have top-secret clearance, don't you?"

"Yes, but why do you ask and who is this man with you, he looks familiar."

"Sorry, this is Captain Billy Norman, recently head of utility department, but he and I now work for the O.S.S. out of Washington. And through them and with the President's permission, I must include you in a hush-hush problem we have here now."

"Vail take a seat, my knees are knocking and I gotta sit down." They sat, the Marshall, continued.

"Now tell me about this hush-hush!"

Bud told him the full story as he understood, but first he swore the U. S. Marshall in as a member of the O.S.S. Studying Davis face he noticed a certain amount of anger in his eyes. "Is there anything you have on your mind Wayne?"

"Yes, it's about the Bait Shop, we've been investigating "Big Shine" on laundering money. I can shut him down and arrest him because I do have enough evidence to bring him in, but I've hesitated due to his autistic son. The boy needs daily attention and I've not found a place for him to receive this."

"What about a state-supported home for him?"

"That should be the last resort. The Negley family are the best alternative since they are number one, his maternal family and number two, the only family he has. Another place would be a teacher that volunteers to teach him basics. She loves him dearly, and Big Shine would approve of her over the Negley family. Probably, with his insistence, a federal judge would approve this move."

"I need this done now. Shut this place down and don't tear it down. Remove all products inside. Seal property off and have it fenced. Place the boy wherever a fed judge approves. Arrest Big and put him away for a while, before a trial. Should he beat the court's decisions in the trial and later return home, let him have the place and his son back. Our purpose is for security reasons. Incidentally, you and I will be in contact daily. If I'm tied up for some reason, Billy can answer and proceed without me. Do you understand ?

Before they left, Bud and Billy were also sworn in as U. S. Marshalls. This would be their cover to procure without revealing their official "big" job with the O.S.S.

With the badges, the two men left to procure items needed. Billy went to law enforcement offices and received captured weapons and ammunition. Bud sent some of his men that worked for him to different boat builders and carpenters to find the necessary boats. He called the manager of Sears and Roebuck, and ordered sufficient sized outboard motors. He also ordered fishing tackle and clothing for the men. He was told it would be a week before order would be fulfilled. He bought a larger motor for Billy Ray's boat. And he sent a veteran boat builder to re-condition the boat. He ordered from a Tuscumbia food store, enough food for a week for amount of men that must be fed.

Billy and he, the next day, went to suspected sites of the dam and nitro plant that could hold explosives. Guide T. V. A. employees quizzically allowed them to study the face of the dam from each side. No revelation as why they were there emitted.

Marshall Davis and his men on the third day after being sworn in, entered the bait shop and arrested Big Shine for money laundering and counterfeiting. He left in a fit of anger and violence. Above all, it was the loss and future of his son, that upset him. Not deeming himself as a nefarious person was explained many times. Money laundering, he felt was not a crime nor a sin. He knew he'd never counterfeited but did harbor for a friend the machine and tools to do so.

Unfortunately, in his opinion, Little Shine would be sent to live with his mother's family while he would be incarcerated. This upset him so much he wept. Also did Little Shine cry profusely. Customers left upset and the events would be in the evening papers and radio.

The Negleys entered upon the movement of Big Shine and collected the crushed little Shine. They called him Gabriel, his official name and one that he didn't answer to. They called him, Gabby.

CHAPTER
FOURTEEN

A parachute jump was made in the cleared jungle by the Nazi commandos and it was uneventful except for the native people who looked, into the heavens as men floated down, in awe.
That night, camping out in the open, a roll call was made as to where the planeload of people would be assigned. Ian would go to Northwest Alabama to destroy a dam and a nitrogen plant with many of his friends. That night, under the stars, he reflected on past, present and future. In the past as a child, student and young man that admired America. Presently, the job he'd recently been trained for, that would kill many of Americans, and he would be in grave danger. In the future, could they escape after the mission was completed. He just had a lot of misgivings.

Boarding the U-Boat, did present problems though. Ian, for one was just too tall. Food was not very good, coffee and tea minimum, nothing to do really. Ian studied the maps of where they were to attack. Their leader spoke of the spy living there. In jest told of the very large man who through negotiations, convinced the brass to give him a "wife", a beautiful Jewess, for him in the United States. Rumor had it that they "promised' her that if she would go, she could leave the ghetto, and her family would be sparred.

They did practice their English and watched American movies. They especially liked Humphry Bogart movies and laughed at his lisp. After such a long journey, they were so glad to get off in the night at Mobile Bay in the Gulf of Mexico. Paddling in rubber rafts, they reached the beautiful white sands and drug the crafts to area between the dunes and buried them.

Strolling in the moonlight, they made their way to the railroad tracks. Spreading out they surveyed the freight and coal cars to learn their destinations. Looking for one that was in-route to the coal digs and mines around Jasper, Alabama became the quest. On a spur, they found one and Jumped on board the coal car. It was empty and clean, so they brought inside with

Boarding the U-Boat, did present problems though. Ian, for one was just too tall. Food was not very good, coffee and tea minimum, nothing to do really. Ian studied the maps of where they were to attack. Their leader spoke of the spy living there. In jest told of the very large man who through negotiations, convinced the brass to give him a "wife", a beautiful Jewess, for him in the United States. Rumor had it that they "promised' her that if she would go, she could leave the ghetto, and her family would be sparred.

They did practice their English and watched American movies. They especially liked Humphry Bogart movies and laughed at his lisp. After such a long journey, they were so glad to get off in the night at Mobile Bay in the Gulf of Mexico. Paddling in rubber rafts, they reached the beautiful white sands and drug the crafts to area between the dunes and buried them.

Strolling in the moonlight, they made their way to the railroad tracks. Spreading out they surveyed the freight and coal cars to learn their destinations. Looking for one that was in-route to the coal digs and mines around Jasper, Alabama became the quest. On a spur, they found one and Jumped on board the coal car. It was empty and clean, so they brought inside with until they by-passed many buildings there.

According to their maps, an ice plant would be last building for about a mile. In the mid-cliff was a small cave they could enter. This they did and found the cave presently and all went in. Once inside, they built a fire and very soon cooked some food. Captain Beck looked around and began counting his men. Did it again, same result. He was missing someone, and he determined it was corporal Ian von Ingalls.

"Do any of you people know where Ingalls is?"

They looked around and shook their heads.

"Who was with him on the coal cars?" Asked Captain Beck. "I was" replied Private Derrick.

"Well when was the last time you saw him?"

He gulped and said, "We jumped together, but he went on down to the bottom of the gully. By the time I slid down the slag and arrived at the bottom, I looked all around but he wasn't there. I assumed he'd moved on out so didn't give it another thought."

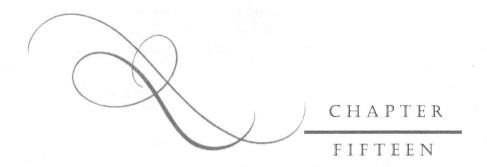

CHAPTER

FIFTEEN

Once he crossed the Tennessee River bridge and entered Florence, he walked up a slope and on the right side of the road he saw the building that held George's Meat Store and direct behind it was a small bungalow with smoke coming out of the chimney.

Beck went around to the back side of the meat store and hid by a wood stockpile and scoped out the residence and waited. Within thirty minutes, an extremely good-looking woman appeared. Jet black long hair, heavenly blue eyes, beautiful body covered by a white apron, with the most beautiful face he'd ever seen. In her arms was a clothes basket filled with white clothes. She started walking toward him, but he felt she hadn't seen Beck yet. Just as she got within a yard, he spoke to her in German. "Vas is los- fraulein?" Startled, she jumped but maintained composure. "Zumir" she asked. "Who is the man?" He asked. She formed an O with her lips. "Zuhause" and walked on in the meat shop, closed door and locked it.

Presently, George Amis appeared. Reverting to English for security reasons, Beck asked.

"George Amis, my name is Beck. Understand you've been waiting on me."

Amis starred at him for a long time before he answered in the affirmative.

"Yah Beck, follow me." They went back to the house where they dissected the orders and Beck learned the physical outline of the mission. Amis, in German, read the plan of attack. Pictures, maps and pistols were available. He loaded up the weapons and could smell the terrific aroma of fried sausage and American homemade biscuits that his "wife" had made and loaded them also. Taking a cardboard box, he loaded up all items. In addition, when the dynamite arrived from Chicago, he'd take his meat truck and drive to the south bank of the river and deliver on a road next to the highway. Beck was directed to have a crew in that area tomorrow sunset to unload. A little confusing but in their language, it all made sense.

IIe departed down the slope, carrying the box and looked back at the shop. Standing in the window looking at him was "Mrs. Amis." She was more beautiful now.

He carried the heavy box under the bridge and located his men. They were very hungry and consumed the food in the box. He told them to follow him and climbed the area by the highway and disappeared into the woods. They followed a path deeper into the area until they found a wooden box covered with vines. Pistols and ammo given to them seemed to grant more confidence in the mission. Opening the box, they found canned food, water, clothes, T.V.A-helmets, and flashlights. Looking now like a maintenance crew, they hid the box, covered and continued.

Soon they came up on an abandoned house, but rather than occupy it, went around to the back where they located a civil war artillery compound with deep slits in the soil. Old fire-pit seem to seek them to build a fire in it and they did. It was in the middle of the perimeter overlooking the river to their north and blocked by many big trees on the south. Unless you were looking for it, you'd not be aware it was there. Ideal place for their camp. The slits would be sleeping area. After unloading what they had in one of the slits, they established another two to be places where they would hide the explosives.

It had been determined to do the drilling of the face of the dam and string lines, in the night, hours. They would begin tonight, incognito with the T. V. garb and helmet on. Using the star manual bits and heavy hammers, tonight would make things ready.

However, it started to rain, and they slept under the floors of the bungalow-chilled. Two men, even in the rain, got a lot done. Problem was, they needed stronger lights to make sure they were getting the job done. Hopefully, no one could see them.

They set up a "watch patrol" and cleaned their weapons. If captured, they were taught, don't give up. Instead kill as many Americans as possible. Escape as soon as possible. They were also taught go south and head for Florida where they would be picked up by another U-Boat.

ACROSS THE RIVER ON THE ISLAND

But, they were seen. On duty, for the Alabama boys, was Bones. Looking through his high-powered binoculars, he saw them begin the drilling and zoomed in to make out they just were too military looking to do this type of work. He woke Billy Ray up for him to check the situation out. He concurred with Bones, but the rain prevented them to do anything tonight.

Something would have to be done though in combating the heavy rain. Flooding could be a bigger problem. They had connected small into big tents to cover them. Protected their weapons and ammo under turned over boats they had brought mid-island. Tomorrow a decision would be made. But, for the night, they would just scan the Nazi. They knew this: Nazi had shut down tonight due to weather. Count was four people so far. They knew not where their camp was, but it had to be on the trails area. T. V. A. people must be blocked from entering this area. Nazi would murder them.

Rains diminished the next day, giving Billy Ray and his men time to rally. A look-see was needed on the south bank and it had to be done now. Looking around at his men, he saw confidence in their eyes when they met with him.

"Here is what I think needs to be done now. We've got to know how many men are over there. So, since Monkey is an accomplished tree climber, and I can sail fair, the two of us will take the skiff and cross over. Hopefully they will think we are just fooling around but we'll go in at the old cotton gin ramp and tie down. We'll then go up and find a tall tree and Monkey should be able to climb high enough to get a count. Figure they are hiding and sleeping during the day and drilling and placing explosives in the holes at night. Don't know where and how they are stringing wire, or setting up another plunger at the nitro plant or the plunger they are planning on using at the dam is powerful enough. Once we learn this data, a decision can be made for today here are ya'lls assignments. Doughbelly, you and spider go ashore and call Bud Goodloe. Ask him if the Angry-5 and batteries are here yet. If so, ya'll collect them and bring them back to the island. Rex, you and Eddie, go ashore and cross the dam You'll need to walk. Go on over and check out if anything is going on at the Nitro plant.

Pay particular attention to the gates, look for wires that are running from the dam, and could be picked up. A big fire could be seen coming from the island. Looked like the plan was coming together. At least they thought.

Monkey found a tree and climbed it. He saw the Nazi milling around small fires and he counted about thirty men. Doughbelly and Spider got the walki-talki but the problem was only a few batteries. They would need to keep at least two charged and there was no electricity to do so. Wisely, they went to U. S. Marshalls office and plugged in. They also left an extra unit with them so that they could communicate in the event it was deemed necessary. And to make matters worse, the island fires went out.

Back at the base of the 'hill' they untied the skiff and floated downstream to McFarland Bottom before they started the motor, then turned around and headed east back to the island and the dam. On the way back; Billy Ray was silent trying to establish a sure-fire plan to capture the Nazi.

They arrived and were proud to learn- that Pepper and little Red had gone ashore and salvaged dry wood and string twine they found in boxes that were discards from the knitting factorie They had even built a bar pique with a spit and had some pork cooking. The smell would attract the Nazi to feel content that no one was watching them and reveal more their mission. But there was more to be done and Billy Ray knowing God was the answer had an idea.

After all of the "Kudzu Kids" met with Billy Ray then begin to be relieved of their anxiety when he answered Doughbelly's question

"Ain't you skeered of all of this going on. Our plans I guess are gone or do you have other?"

Billy Ray mused for a while and then answered

"Yes I'm a little bit afraid. But I, like you, have received the best military training for this type of mission and that relieves me a lot. Now let me give you a plan that Napoleon had before he went into battle. Here's what he said "First we go up there and then we'll see what happens".

Bones spoke up and asked

"Who is Napoleon"?

Billy Ray grinned and answered

"He was a French Dictator and General" the group just looked at him.

Bones again "What's the difference between a Frenchman and a frog"?

Doughbelly took his cap off and hit him on his head several times.

"Quit asking dumb questions all the time" he said; to which Bones answered

"Just trying to learn sumptin".

Each man laughed loudly at such antics. Billy Ray then put a straight face on and said "The plan is this: Just like football plays.

Once we come in the area headed toward the dam, we'll see a truck. You go over there and take charge of it, Doughbelly. Allow no one except us to enter or leave it. Containment in the bed of it will be their weapons and ammo. Take the machine gun with you. Lock and load as soon as you arrive. Protect yourself by setting up behind a forked tree near the truck. Noticed it the other night when I scouted the place. Camouflage.

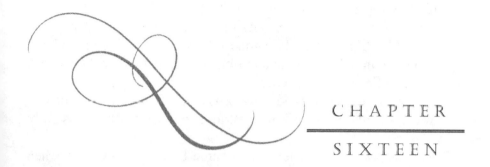

CHAPTER

SIXTEEN

"Doughbelly", he whispered to his friend, walk with me to the bank." Of course, they did so that their voices wouldn't be heard.

"What's up?" he asked

Billy Ray replied,

"It's this way, I've counted the number of people they have and we're greatly out-numbered. Granted we can stop them, but no way can we capture them. So, got an idea. We need some people to stop them on the south side and I think I can get some help from "Ples" and his people. All they will have to do is knock them down and hold them until we get there. Ples' people don't have any weapons but they have a lot of strength and agility and if they are willing, this is what I should do. After all, they are Americans, even if our law says they can't be in combat. Sounds like a stupid General made that law up anyway. What do you think?"

"Bring me up to date on Ples?"

"Don't you remember, he's colored and now a bishop in the A.M. & church. We grew up together and escaped from the Masonic Home for boys, down in Columbus, Mississippi. He had folks here, but I couldn't live with them, but stayed in the warehouse that Mr. Ware had built to store cotton-bales, until Bud Goodloe found me and gave me a home at Pride's Landing."

"Yea, I recall now. Not bad idea. But, how you gonna get with him?"

"His church is just over near the area of the Nitro plant. I'm going to cross stream and edge around the buildings and try to find him. I'll leave now. Don't tell anyone. Get back in the morning sometime, I reckon."

With that, he left on the skiff and floated downstream to the southbank near the bridge and tied down and hidden. He was thinking how he missed "Lucy", his jack Russell dog. She was with jane, Bud's fiancé and he knew she was being well protected. As he climbed the bank and started his trek toward the village where Ples lived, he couldn't help but remember growing up with him. His real name was Pleasant but was called most of his life as Ples. He'd gone to high school at Trenholm High and graduated with honors, enough to obtain a scholarship to Alabama A & M in Huntsville, Alabama, where he majored in religious studies and did all of work necessary to make it as a Bishop. This was due, to the fact that he was a negro and wasn't allowed to attend same schools as Billy Ray.

But they were dear friends and came to each other's aid when needed. Pleasew was also very patriotic and would go to military service if they would let him serve as a Chaplain. He needed Ples now, but more important, his country did. Ples had always called him "Fishbait", he grinned at that and then remembered since thinking about nicknames, that the code name for this mission and especially his men was "Kudzu". He would need to use that name more often.

Coming up on the cabin where Ples lived, he went around to the back and knocked on the door and said "Plesss", to which a voice answered, "Fishbait?"

"Yea man, let me in before one of your parishioners cuts my throat."

Door was open by a big black man with a superb smile and a hug for his childhood friend.

"What are you doing here, Billy Ray."

"Aw just needed a good cup of coffee for a change."

Ples poured him one and added sugar, just the way he liked it.

"Naw, what you really doing here?"

"Need help."

"What else is new?"

"This is not as personal as usual, this concerns us all"

With that, Billy Ray told the story as best he could without giving away too much.

"What can I do, or better still, my villagers."

"Need a dozen men to get in a horseshoe position under cover and wait until my men flush the enemy out of the south gate of the nitrogen plant. Do this at research 501 field. Keep things silent, tell your men to do the same, no rumors or else the whole population will be here just getting in the way."

"What about politicians or law-enforcement?"

"Bud will handle that when we learn proper time arises. U. S. Marshalls are in on this and will be great help. T. V. A., employees, other than the top-management are unaware of the crisis."

"How will I be informed?"

"Will get you a walki-talki and how to use it from one of my men, as soon as possible."

With that Billy Ray departed same way as he came in. Slight difference, he entered the woods at the face of the dam to seek information if possible. Two men were hammer-drilling lightly.

He back-tracked to look-over if any wires were on the ground leading to the Nitrogen plant. Yes, he noted four were laying in a tight pattern and pushed under a fence. Mud was spread as if someone had tried to climb the eight-footer. Something was going on and he didn't like it.

Continuing, he went down the hill, mostly sliding, then found the skiff. Crossing the river with motor running, he entered the old canal and went east on it bumping into logs and roots, and able to enter in a slew and back into the river when he arrived at island site. Tied down with just a mist in the air he was tired and sought some food along with dry clothes.

CHAPTER
SEVENTEEN

He got back to the island and inquired what they had seen. Billy Ray went to the "soup kitchen" and got a big bowl of okra gumbo with crackers and lemonade. Pretty good food for riverside cooking. As he ate he thought. New idea about when they would attack. He'd been informed that nothing " concrete" to report except a considerable flashlight show as if they were looking for something. This told him that it was a good possibility that wiring was being laid and that they would be working at night instead of daylight and hid somewhere during day time.

Regardless, he and the squad would go in tomorrow night. This was the United States of America, home of the free and the brave and this enemy had been in this country too long. "Kudzu" would stay in place and wait until tomorrow and make their move. He called them together and explained what they would do. It was agreeable to the guys on using the "colored" as Billy Ray wanted. Just hope and pray he doesn't get in trouble over it.

THE ATTACK

Preparation for war is one thing, but actually doing it is the most terrifying event you'll ever experience. The men also known as "Kudzu Kids" were calm professional soldiers of the earth and the sea. Yet the former "Hillbillies" were on a track that unknowingly would bring them fame someday. Being former concrete-finishers, they learned when the time called for a job that must be finished right, patience and hard work were the keys. This was the profundity of their soul. This what they must do tonight.

Bones had already brought his armed for combat boat around the island and set pointed toward the enemy. He had added an anchor with cable in case he needed it. The vessel was camouflaged with tree branches that Bones hoped the enemy would think was a floating tree berg. Remainder of the squad loaded up with weapons and themselves. Ammo was attached to their body. They would lock and load when they made land on the other side.

Across the powerful Tennessee they went with their leader whom they had all respect and had confidence. They were so sure of him and his positive ways that it had "rubbed" off on them.
He said a quick prayer and pulled the trigger on the flare-gun, like a blast of sunshine that maintained a beautiful glow and arc. Captain Beck looked up, spotted Ensign Coleman with his .45 drawn and then pulled his 9mm Luger out and fired at him and missed. Ensign Coleman didn't. As Beck was leaving this life, his last thought was "where is Ian von Ingalls".

To his left the barrage began. It was evident both groups were highly trained and hoisted their weapons to fire at each other, but a skinny boy from Tuscumbia, Alabama, created a no bloodbath war miracle. Bones sped forward in a straight line toward the melee. When he got to the designated area to drop anchor on a pile of rocks, a sudden swirl spun him away from this safety area and moved him to open water. The anchor dropped and must have connected with an old tree log that locked him into a frozen position. He partially stood and turned to look back, when he slipped and fell face forward in the boat. Falling he caught the firing mechanism of the .30 caliber machine gun. This caused the barrel to be pointed almost skyward. In his haste, he accidentally pushed down the button and began firing. The locked position plus the momentum of the firing non-stop weapon put Bones and his boat into an action of gravity called a pendulum. This force caused irregular firing of the machine gun.

Bones somehow had wedged his arm and hand and couldn't or wouldn't attempt to do anything. Anxiety had got the best of him and little did he know that his firing the machine gun was going through the top of the trees where 'Kudzu" and "Nazi" were fighting.
The Germans thought a large group of excellent soldiers were firing at them from the river. No one was in charge so they started as if on an escape and evasion exercise, running southward and shooting back at

the pursing Americans.

Later it was described as watching an old cops and robbers b-rated movie. No one was wounded or injured. Only one fatality, Captain Becir.

The Germans ran directly into the residents of "Uniontown" and they were waiting for them. All were captured, interrogated, and tied up. They talked freely about their sabotage organizations after they learned they would go to an American P.O.W. camp.

By the time Billy Ray and his squad arrived on Research road where the Germans were being held captive did he learn that his tactics of using the men of Uniontown was successful.

The Germans were tied up with strips of cotton cloth that the ladies of Uniontown had contributed with their commitment. Standing guard over the huddled captives was Morris with his famous .410 double barrel. His entire body was in a clinch. Billy Ray walked up to him, put his arm around and relieved him of the shotgun and sent him to his village group for an overdue welcome. He assembled his own people and began giving assignments. The first one was to go back to the attack site and bring Bones and his arsenal up from the shore. They were to take funeral directors to Wilson dam to retrieve Nazi officer's body. He wanted Billy Norman get in touch with T.V.A., management and bring them in on tonight's actions and have them go with proper people to search the entire area for possible buried land mines, and other explosives. The proper people would be sent up from Fort McClellan's bomb squad. Police that showed up were dispatched by Billy Ray to remove the captives and jail them in the basement of the Sheffield Jail. Bud Goodloe wearing his U.S.M.C. uniform was officer in charge and he came down hard on media representatives and nosy by- standers.

Colonel Bud Goodloe U.S.M.C. (reserves), began the process of security. He assembled the Sheriff of Colbert County and his deputies with him and announced "those of you that are not with the press or radio, must leave at once. You will be patrolled by the Sheriff's department and exited from this area.

What happened here tonight is not any of your business. We are at war and you can't participate in any way here. Now leave"! The deputies escorted them to their vehicles while listening to a lot of complaints.

Ples and the people of Uniontown returned home waiting for Billy

Ray to appear and give them a report on activities.

Billy Norman was back at his office making phone calls to people that needed to know what had occurred. Army personnel were alerted for arrival in the morning of their demolishment personnel to clear the attack zone.

Bud upon receiving clarification from Billy Ray, word was sent to General Bill Donovan and gave him the good news. The President of the United states was immediately Informed and conveyed to Donovan his deepest congratulations to the men who made this happen. He also told him to pass back down that this was hush-hush.

Bud pulled the media aside and gave them their "orders". "Gentlemen, it's this way, what you saw tonight and what you heard tonight will stay here. You are not allowed to print, air or lecture about it. This is a direct order from the President. His words and I quote "should anyone of the media release this top-secret information, their license to operate will be revoked at once". Bud again "This is not a violation of any article. Should you take issue, proceed with lawsuit but I warn you, any violation toward the President of the United States, for any reason could result in your permanent closure of the business you represent and you'll be jailed.

Disbelief would describe their expression. The disc jockey that had been sent to cover this event for radio started to announce over his microphone something, when Bud knocked him to the ground and took away his microphone, discorded it and gave it back to the startled young man. "We mean it people" he shouted at them. They departed at once.

T.V.A., security guards were sent to guard the attack area, especially where the dynamite had been dropped.

Billy Ray gathered his men, loaded them up and took off for "Uniontown" to celebrate with those that helped them.

CHAPTER
EIGHTEEN

Bud contacted Billy Ray on the "Walki-Talki" and asked him to load his men up from the "jubilee" and bring them to the Sheffield hotel. Their rooms would contain necessary hygiene articles including fresh underwear. Bud had put all of the people that worked for him on duties to make life for the coast guardsmen to be more pleasant. The dining room was opened and piles of bacon-lettuce-tomato sandwiches were available plus sweet ice tea and to cap it off, pecan pie ala-mode.
He then set Billy Ray down and talked to him about Gloria.

"It's like this: I know you are dying to see Gloria but that can't happen. She's not available."

The world suddenly turned black for Billy Ray.

"I don't understand, he said, Is she dead"?

Bud saw in his eyes something just above terror.

"No", Bud quickly answered, "She's married and gone from this area. She's also pregnant."

Billy Ray became uncontrollable. This strong willed man lost it and was racked with tears. He just looked at Bud, trying to find an answer and asked "who"

Bud grimly answered

"Reverend Rayford Dennis. You've been directed to report to General Donovan and get this, later on to the President of the United States."

Billy Ray tried to be cool about it but he felt his knees start quivering. All he could mutter was "Explain".

Bud started laughing profusely,

"You should see your face"! Billy Ray had endured a lot today and

70

he didn't believe he could take much more. "Please" was all he could say.

"All right then, here are your orders and I'll explain in military terms and metaphors.

1. A barber will be here soon to give you an officer's haircut.
2. In the morning at 05:30 a jeep will pick you up. Be fresh shaven, showered, shampooed and ready to travel.
3. You'll be taken to Courtland Army Air Force, to a four engine plane that will take you to Washington. To greet you will be Colonel Donovan. By the way, you'll be flying in the President's personal plane and I'm told it is fancy.

On board will be his traveling staff. You'll eat on board. In addition, on board will be Colonel Donovan's private secretary. Her job is to listen and do shorthand about all that occurred from the time ya'll arrived from the Poconos until now. Leave out the part concerning Gloria. Be detailed. Even the part about Bones, Yes I've already heard about his contribution. Hey! Did you know he got wounded? It was a 9mm slug, caught it on his bony shoulder. 5. On board will be an ensign class-a uniform. Shined shoes, tie, white shirt, officer's hat and a portfolio file briefcase. These are yours. Normally an officer's uniform isn't given to him, but in this case, no charge. Re-shave in the lavatory of the plane when you learn where you are after giving your dictation. Upon completion of your information, the secretary will go, I'm sure, into another area to type reports for the President, Colonel Donovan, You, and of course, file.
6. Address the President as: Mr. President, President, Sir or nothing
7. Follow the General's lead.
8. Thank them at any opportunity. Use manners I've taught you.
9. You'll spend the night on the President's yacht. You'll be fed and have a place to shower etc. Wear pajamas on board, ladies are subject to enter and leave.
10. On board will be boxes of uniforms, pay, files, important documents, and new weapons/ammo. Office equipment along with a patrol boat, lights, etc. for river patrol. You must continue your diligent duty from the new Wheeler dam all the way to Pickwick.
11. Your men will bivouac at the T.V.A. apartment near Tuscumbia Landing on Spring creek. Your new detachment building will be completed soon.
BILLY RAY'S PRAYER

"Lord, I know that you will always be my Father. I know how to live right because you taught me. Bless you for the many ways you love me, and thank you for the many ways you've blessed me. But, Lord, I don't understand about Gloria. How could she do me this way? Was her love for me so shallow? Did you reveal to her that your minister was sent here was the one for her and not me? Put into my heart the right way to handle this, please, oh God. I still hurt so much but I know it's not in vain. Father please give both of us peace and understanding. Bless her husband. Now Father as I travel to Washington, be with my men. Bless the events coming up that I will be understanding and do the tasks you've bestowed on me with strength, compassion and Love. Lord, let me live in your walk as long as you ordain it. I love you Lord. Amen."

The two officers were marched in by four honor guards to the President's office. The General's family, Commander Thomas Moody from New London, and military and political pundits like Secretary of the Army, Secretary of the Navy, Secretary of State, Secretary of War and the Vice-President. Various photographers including the President's own, plus important Senators and Congressmen. Standing next to the President was Senator Lister Hill, Democrat from Alabama, were in attendance.

Smiles were abundant. The active military personnel joined behind General Donovan and hand-saluted upon command, the commander-in-chief, who less-military like, saluted them. They took two steps back and went to parade rest. One of the honor guards taught Billy Ray this before he entered the oval office.

He was impressed by only two people present when he entered. President Roosevelt and Senator Lister Hill. The President, Senator Hill, and Secretary Stinson, beamed at the Ensign as he was ushered to stand in front of the President and wait until other formalities were conducted. Specifically, the official promotion of Donovan to General. Roosevelt did his usual flowers 'n sweets speech about the newly promoted General. Then it was the young Alabamian who would benefit. Actually, he didn't think a promotion would be granted. After all, he'd just graduated at New London.

"You know Ensign Coleman, I consider I'm an old salt. The Coast Guard, like the Navy are seaman, and that is not easy duty. However, when you take the seaman and place him on land and tell him to fight, it takes a lot of desire from him to be successful. From reports I have, you could be successful either way. I concur and am of the belief that rewords are in order. Therefore, I'm going to promote you to Lieutenant junior grade and place you as officer-in-charge of an attachment. This is a permanent promotion. In accordance with position promotion, and since you are serving also with the office of strategic services, I shall use my prerogative as President of the United States and promote you to Lieutenant. In addition, you are awarded the bronze star and even if you are sea personnel, the combat infantry badge, normally for the Army, will be presented to you and your men. The people of Uniontown will also receive some accommodations. Thank you son, for what you do." Billy Ray, with tears in his eyes, saluted did an about face.

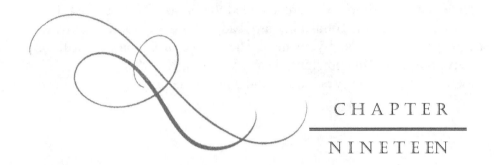

CHAPTER

NINETEEN

The truck had been unloaded when he arrived home. He had been assigned a single apartment in T.V.A complex in village # 1. This was a village of stucco houses with tile roofs, complete with electric range and refrigerator.

His apartment was nice also. Ceiling fans, large living room, bedroom with regular sized bed and feather mattress. Dinette in kitchen area that contained range and refrigerator. Soon he'd get some more furniture and hopefully a radio. Eddie had set on his front door several boxes with his name on it. After mysteriously finding another key in the door, he entered and brought the boxes in and unloaded them. Mostly beautiful class a uniforms, caps and hats, top coat, ties, white shirts, dungaree uniforms and just about anything he'd need.

He arranged the room in order to accommodate his men to come in to see him. He stepped out in the hall and saw Rex and asked him to gather up the guys and come to his apartment # 607.
All of the squad gathered in his room and they had a small party.
"Gosh it's good to see you. Bring me up to date" asked Billy Ray. Doughbelly started first.
"Bud er uh Colonel Goodloe has been taking care of us. Showed us this place, had keys for each. Arranged gas for the truck, fed us, and let us get some rest. Little Red was next,"
We went without anyone telling us back to where our boats were and brought them here."
Pepper, "I brought your boat here also." Rex chirped,"Brought the

gas cans back also".

Spider spoke bluntly "Tell us about your trip" Billy Ray looked them over and saw concern on their faces. He began as quietly as he could. He saw strange looks when he told them about Gloria. Anger, sadness, tears, all the emotions you could muster came out. Awe was the word when he told them about meeting the President. Glee when he told them of the promotion.

"Friends I've got some news that's going to knock you for a loop, they gave me permission and the power to promote each of you to E-3 rank, except Doughbelly and his will be E-4, NCOIC. I need someone that the Coast guard will approve and I know if I give him an assignment, it will be carried out.

"Saved the best for last----If I can find a manual typewriter, tomorrow I'll send recommendations for all of you to receive the congressional unit citation, naval commendation medal, your shooting badges, and the navy bronze star. In addition, in each of your files, letter of Appreciation, letter of commendation and Bones will receive a purple heart for injuries received when he got hit by a 9mm from a luger". At first the guys started smiling and then realized Bones had been the butt of too many jokes, so they refrained.

"Tell me about our headquarters". Little Red spoke up and told him about the size of each room. "Room size office for staff, your office a little smaller, kitchen, day room, and weapons room. Two exits and a lot of big windows. Sign is being hung today, we need to paint and build some shelves. Need typewriters, desks, chairs, and office supplies." Billy Ray studied on the situation and asked "Red, would you consider going back to school and learn how to type? We need a detachment clerk." Red seemed to like the idea and agreed to do this.

Billy Ray ventured out on some plans that included all of this staff to learn how to pilot, do mechanical, fire cannon, treat the vessel correctly; and in short become a master seaman on patrol boats.

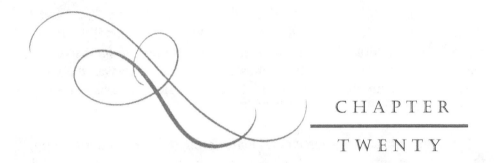

CHAPTER

TWENTY

A year had passed, and the detachment maintained top efficiency. The promotions and awards were made. Little Red graduated from typing school at the top of his class. He was the only male and that helped him overcome his shyness. He ran the office almost perfect. The building was impeccable. Painted battle ship gray inside and out.
The patrol boat arrived and the Tennessee was a perfect place to learn navigation. His crew to the man, were able to take any boat out for any reason and complete the task. Jeep, car and a small truck was added to the detachments inventory.

Billy Ray always wanted more for his men. He inquired about the CFA program, in order; to educate them for promotions. When he was turned down for this, he figured they would be reassigned for combat situations. He was right. On a cloudy Monday, he went to the post office to retrieve their mail. He noticed a large envelope that had been taped down. When he opened it; his worst fears overcame. The entire detachment force was being reassigned and not collectively.

Reading the assignment orders was more dramatic than he thought it would be. As he read, sadness was beginning to enter his soul, not as much as when he got the information about Gloria but so dreadful.
Doughbelly was being assigned to a large coast guard unit in England, Pepper to temporary duty in security located at Pickwick dam and then he too would be assigned to England. The Adams brothers to San Diego for more training and then to the Far East Command. Little Red to Department of the Navy in Washington. Spider also would enter security and sent to Memphis Naval Yard. Monkey had requested and approved to attend

marine officer school at Parris Island. Bones ended up with the choicest assignment. He would be an instructor back at New London with a rank promotion. He'd met a lovely little lady, Carolyn Austin, and now they could wed and live off base in the quaint little city.

Telling them goodbye would be the hardest farewell he'd ever do. Welcoming a new squad would be a new experience.
He'd followed up on the people involved in the attack. The federal judge sent the German prisoners to Jasper, Alabama's prisoner of war camp. Their duties were as coal miners.

George Amis was convicted of murder and sent to Federal prison somewhere and executed.
"Sue" was cleared of all charges and was granted asylum. She lived with "Sissy"
Goodloe at the serene
"Pride's Landing". Billy
Ray sponsored her and Sissy as if she had a new doll to play with, clothed, styled, taught her English, and was the matchmaker for she and Billy Ray.

Billy Ray visited a lot of the sites in his area. Frequently, to Uniontown, where through his influence, had Senator Hill to push the T.V.A. management to build new houses, pave streets and sidewalks, plant landscape vegetation, place post office and a doctor's office there.

Proper water and sanitation was a must and was done first class. The bait shop was beginning to fall on hard times. "Hard Case" who worked for Mr. Shine for many years was killed in a barroom brawl. "Little Shine" seem to get even larger, and needing close supervision, had to be placed with a permanent caregiver and removed from the river bank. The swift waters now prevented fishermen to "put in" here.

Most of the young men that were his good customers, had been drafted or joined the military. All of this, allowed the decision to close and he took a job of driving a truck, hauling meats. Billy Ray never saw Gloria again. He did go by and checked in on her Grandparents. They were not friendly anymore about Gloria. Love to talk about the time he'd taken them to Nashville for the Grand Old Opry, and that was about it.
Still love to visit the old camp site at "Pride's Landing" and reminisce about his days there. Bud the great concierge and master at organizing was now special military aide to the Governor. He'd been the most important person in his life. But even he didn't know "Where is Ian Von Ingalls?"

CHAPTER
TWENTY-ONE

Lieutenant Billy Ray Coleman, U.S.C.G., had shipped the last of his original detachment of Coast Guardsmen, to participate more- or-less in combat, during the middle of World War Two, from Tuscumbia Landing in Northwest Alabama to parts all over doing fighting.

Being divided in duties, either in Coast Guard or O.S.S., the word all ways came down from Washington. He'd waited several weeks, but nothing happened. He caught himself teaching or correcting the replacements from his friends that had served with him as they captured Nazi commandos from exploding Wilson Dam and the adjacent Nitrogen plant, that were part of the Tennessee Valley Authority. located on the Tennessee River. After all the training, the war he'd endured, living on a creek bank wasn't exactly his idea of serving his country.

He still lived in the officer's bachelor's quarters at the government owned billets and was driving the gray jeep issued to him by the Coast guard.

The lady he'd loved for most of his life, starting as a teen on up to a few years ago, was over. She'd wed and moved to Mississippi to serve churches as a pastor's wife. He had not talked nor seen her from day that he departed to enter the Coast Guard. He saw her Grandparents at the A & P from time to time, but very little conversation with them.

He visited at "Pride's Landing" checking on "Sissy", Bud Goodloe's sister and her house guest, Sue. She is known as the "wife' of George Amis, the butcher spy that formulated the attempt on exploding the river structures. Her correct name was Heidi, and she was here because being a Jew would be obligated to the Nazi back in Germany that would exterminate her upon first sight. She was told by Himmler that if she traveled with

78

Heir Amis, pose as his wife, her family would be exonerated from the concentration camps and they would be joined again when she returned. Why she believed Himmler no one could understand.

Billy Ray found her to be beautiful with a great personality and smile. They spent time in teaching each other their native tongues. He took her on a date once and they saw "Gone with the Wind", she was fascinated with the "old south," that she learned from the epic movie.

Billy Ray got a phone call one Sunday, directing him to drive for nearby Fort McClellan, Alabama to meet with his O.S.S.

"Today. But I need you to go early and investigate a rumor that U-boats are going up-stream on the Mississippi river. Let me know what you learn. Use the enigma I sent you. After a time spent on board of a cutter, I'll relieve you and you're to return to your home. I'll reassign you then"

"Aye-Aye sir"

"Now head back and pack only coast guard issued clothing. "

"Sir, do you know what my duties will be on the Cutter?"

"You'll be the skipper. It's about time. Here is the code book for the enigma. Study the usage manual when you have time to study alone. Do one dummy message. Lieutenant Carolyn, who works for me will return a message. Take it with you when you go sailing with the coast guard".

"Aye-Aye sir"

It had been some time since he'd been on a cutter. During his training at New London, he seemed to absorb the details and realized that this was an endeavor he was destined for to be successful. Driving back home, he wondered exactly what his duties would be on the cutter. Nothing had appeared in the newspapers that told him if any war time activity was occurring in the Gulf of Mexico. He did know that the Germans were excellent sailors and they were subject to attacking at any time or anywhere. Could his home port be New Orleans or some town closer to the Gulf?

Later that evening he arrived at his barracks, got a good night' s sleep and reported to Tuscumbia Landing detachment and waiting for him was his replacement, Lieutenant William Garrett, from Chicago, Illinois. They spent the next two days going over job description and meeting his men.

Late on the second day, he had "Sissy" to pick him up for "Pride's Landing" to catch the 8:40 train for Memphis. Bidding him farewell was Heidi, who hugged him as he boarded. Their eyes- locked and both knew something was connecting between them.
She blew him a kiss and he returned one. This could be the start of something grand.

CHAPTER
TWENTY-TWO

He caught the Memphis train to the Millington Naval Yard and then to the Coast Guard Detachment Center. Excitement was worn just as his navy- blue dress uniform, shined shoes, and even shiner medals and badges that he'd earned at the mission of Wilson Dam/Nitrogen battle. His Lieutenant Bars were standing out for all to see. Once he arrived at the train station, he inquired how to get transportation to the proper facilities. After a wait, a young blond petty officer picked him up and gave him a "run-down".

Food was great at the "mess hall" at the Millington facility. All he would need to do was show his ID card. Dry cleaners, movies, snack bars, bank and Memphis opportunities were available. Girls were "Southern Belles" looking for husbands, especially the pilots because they received flight pay. Speaking of pilots and trainee pilots, try to stay away from them or else be prepared to defend yourself. They were so cocky that they would love to brag about how good they were at fist-fighting.

Floor shows with dances happened on Saturday nights. Three churches were available. Catholic, Protestant, and Jewish were just now being completed and Naval leaders of each were due to arrive soon. Bachelor quarters, just for Coast Guard officers, was now available and he'd be dropped off there. Then he was to bring his orders and first, report to Naval Headquarters afterward report to the Coast Guard Detachment.

He did all that he'd been instructed to do without any problems until he reported to the detachment. Upon reporting in, he was asked to meet with the commanding officer. Long wait until Lieutenant Commander F. Abraham Watson, arrived. He came to attention and asked permission to speak to the CO. Permission granted and after door was closed and Billy Ray was asked to sit down, did he learned why he was invited to enter this office.

"Lieutenant, I didn't know our branch of the services held alliance to the O.S.S." stated the officer.

Billy Ray answered with a question,

"What difference would that make and why have you brought this up?"

"Makes no difference to me except if you require anything I'm obligated "answered the CO."

"Sir it's this way, for the time being; I am a Coast Guard officer, ordered to skipper a cutter that I'm doing the first time since New London." Replied Billy Ray

"And that is somewhat of a problem for you. The cutter you're going to board is running at least a week late. It has new mounted ice plows on it and if they can't get them off. You'll have to proceed with them. This cutter has recently been re-outfitted. Here are the detailed modifications, handing him a memo type of description. My understanding the reason you are getting this assignment is due to the excellent scores both educational and manually while at New London. Your command officer, Commander Tom Moody, gave you an outstanding valuation and used the words "has the makings of a future Admiral".

Billy Ray laughed out loud at that choice of words. "You don't know me sir, but if you did, you'd say this guy is the last to be considered for an Admiral." Each man smiled at the other. Then Billy Ray asked the supreme question.

"How are you so familiar with the O.S.S.?"

"Can answer only this way. Notified you were coming and was asked by your O.S.S. commander for you to travel on the banks of the river, going north to learn that if any evidence reveals that a Nazi U-boat, was traveling or has traveled in this direction. South of here has been scanned. No evidence revealed. So, my advice to you would be to go in that direction tomorrow. Go best way you can and be discreet. I'd leave the navy alone on this. Can't understand them on matters such as this."

"Advice will be taken."

"Do I contact O.S.S. and tell them you're here or do you handle notifications. By the way, delivered today was a heavy box for you. Wait later about opening it. Is there anything else you need to know?"

"Yes, the bankers name here on base?" Will do my commo"

"J. S. Cantrell, good man".

"Thank you, sir, will check in with you in two or three days."

"Mighty fine Lieutenant, keep me posted."

When Billy Ray was alone, he opened the box and found an enigma, the safest way of communicating with the O.S.S. Now he must get to the bank as soon as possible and lock this up in the bank's vault.

"Good afternoon sir, my name is Coleman, and I need to open an account with your bank" said Billy Ray.

"Yes sir, Lieutenant, my pleasure. Exactly what do you want?"

"Transfer of funds from my home bank back in Alabama, have your assigned stock market person to take care of my stocks, small checking account and the use of your vault."

"We can do all of that plus advance you cash if you need it now"

"No have cash on me, but if you can, find for me an automobile, a good mechanic, where to buy horse and saddle and a stable to leave the animal while I'm pulling duty."

Mr. Cantrell, pursed his lips and stood up, buttoned his banker's gray double- breasted coat, walked around the office for a little time, began sizing up this Coast Guard officer and asked, "Lieutenant can you tell me what you want to place in my vault?"

"No sir, it is secret and I'm requiring you to keep it that way. Further, if a problem exists and it is after hours and I need these contents, I'll need you to open the vault for me"

"Why not store with the Navy"

'It's personal and my business is not with them, but folks in Washington. Sir I wear two hats and the less people know about me the better. That's why I selected you, a stranger." have your request for transfer of funds and stocks done as soon as you fill-out these papers. Bring what you need to "store" in the vault in about an hour when we close. At that time hope to have some information for you on purchasing the auto and the horse."

Billy Ray complied with the filling in of blanks for the opening of an account, signed, shook Mr. Cantrell's hand and departed to unpack his bags.

After checking out the base and having a meal at the "mess hall", he returned to the bank with the enigma back in its box, hammered shut and non-descript. Mr. Cantrell told him of a farmer that owned a black and white pinto with saddle for sale at a good price. Saddle and tact included all for fifty dollars. He also told him of a mechanic that owned a nineteen forty convertible for sale for a hundred dollars but would need some work done on it. Billy Ray thanked Mr. Cantrell, got directions and left to see about the car first.

CHAPTER
TWENTY-THREE

In order to maintain his energy ; and to deliver his report to O.S.S., he, through the base commander, was allowed to enter the top-secret room to send message about the findings that he'd been instructed to investigate. Using the enigma code machine, all was done easily. He'd need to do this later from war clues he would uncover.

Next, he contacted his banker and arranged for paying funds to whomever took care of the horse when he bought it. He also arranged for knowledge of the investments he made long ago. When the depression ended he began receiving much needed funds from auto-makers, oil, rubber and steel investments. Bud had advised him what to do.
He then went to the docks with bags and baggage waiting for the seen cutter about ten miles upstream. Re-reading his orders revealed common knowledge about this cutter (Coast Guard nomenclature for sea-bearing craft was not boat, ship, or water-craft but cutter). First, it was a WPG (gunboat) 45 named Haida, a Tampa class. It would displace 1955 tons. Length is 240', beam 39', draft 17'9", speed 15 knots. The armament 2-3"/50, 4-20mm, 2 dc tracks, 4-Y-guns, and 2-mousetraps. Amazingly, the diesel-electric engines, had only one screw.

Built in California, it was only 21 years old. The complement was: Ten officers, two warrants, One- hundred enlisted and a full hospital. Through his O.S.S. contacts, the sonar and radar components would be waiting for him to mount in New Orleans. He'd previously flown to Cape May, New Jersey to learn how to pilot this cutter. While there he completed a crash course on sonar and radar and would be officer-in-charge of these machines, once missions were designated. He'd gone to Cape May while at the Academy.

Pilot of the Haida, was a perfectionist and pulled in to shore exactly as he should. The gang- plank was dropped and he went aboard. Meanwhile, fuel tanks were top-off and they were underway with designation, New Orleans.

After proper salutes, credentials and orders presented, he was led on a tour of the deck by an Ensign, apparently a recent Academy graduate, from the way he asked questions that shouldn't be uttered. Taken to his living quarters, he immediately began changing uniforms but before he could take his tunic off, he was addressed by a very young P.O. and gave him Captain's invitation to join him in the officers dining room.

"Lieutenant Billy Ray Coleman, reporting as ordered sir" announced the new officer on deck.

He stood at attention and remained that way until the Cutter Captain finally replied,

"At ease, take a seat".

Billy Ray complied. Immediately the Captain started ranting about how the Germans were the scrounged human on earth and it was his duty to extinguished as many as he could. He spoke very bluntly as he shared that "southern military weren't capable to think on their feet and must be led at any time as to their mission" also that on this cutter no one was to make any decisions except him. Anger was brewing inside Billy Ray.

"Question young man, what did you do to wear the Navy Cross"? Billy Ray stirred the sugar he'd put in his coffee slowly trying to control himself but finally said

"With all respect sir, why do you feel the way you do about southern military men? In addition, why would you not give your crew the opportunity to think for themselves?"

Furthermore, this Navy Cross is legal and presented to me by our commander-in-chief, President Roosevelt. My orders specify that I'm to mount, serve two very important implements, and train enlistees to be able to operate them. Did you not get these same orders sir"?

"How dare you speak the way you just did Coleman, I'm now your commanding officer" yelled Captain Levy. "

Yes sir, you are but why do you disrespect me so much" asked Billy Ray?

Both men calmed down. Billy Ray never took his eyes from him. Levy's hands shook and then spoke "That'll be all, Lieutenant Coleman", Billy Ray stood, rendered an unanswered hand salute, did an about face and exited the main door.

Enlistees in the hall all had heard the quarrel and looked at Billy Ray with respect.
Typical of any military establishment, gossip started. There it was called "scuttlebutt" and soon another Lieutenant knocked on his door. Opening he found the most Irish looking individual he'd ever seen.

"Hiya Billy Ray, my name is Timothy O'Kell'. They shook hands and the infectious grin from Tim caused Billy Ray to return same grin even though he'd just experienced a bad situation.

"Tim, glad to meet you, where you from?" Tim again with the grin "I'm from the south too, as a matter of fact my family and I are called Southies. We are from South Boston".

Billy Ray again grinned bigger and uttered "Either you were asleep during Geography class or you want to be considered as a member of the deep south and known as an elite Johnny Reb. Which is it"? Taking a seat, he made eye contact and said "Neither, just wanted to meet another soul that Levy disliked". Billy Ray gave a sign to continue.

"He fancies the two of us as people he fears. He has no confidence, doesn't know how this cutter operates and depends on CPO Huey Walker to keep us floating and moving. Chief Walker understands him and prevents the enlisted men from crossing paths with the Captain.

He dislikes me since I caught him drunk in his quarters shouting at our cook for serving sandwiches instead a full meal. He actually punched the cook, but I hustled him out of further harm's way and muffled the Captain's drunken disorderly conduct. He is Jewish even though he doesn't go to the temple. Refugee from the Navy, who tried to dry him out. Feels Southern states hate Jews and Colored therefore he is to hate them in return. In short, he needs to be replaced and retired or at least send to do administration work. If you can, request to be transferred.

CHAPTER
TWENTY-FOUR

Arriving at dead of night had become his standard operating procedure. Regardless of the Coast Guard policies and procedures, he knew that in his heart he was O.S.S.

Recently spent six days in New Jersey to be reacquainted with the large Cutters that had recently been distributed to detachments that patrolled the rivers. A larger cutter was already in use along both Coast lines, Great Lakes, Gulf of Mexico, and running along the Texas shore lines. He went to New Jersey after he got news of impending transfer.
Now that Lieutenant Billy Ray Coleman was in Memphis to await arrival of one of the new cutters to transport down to his new assignment in New Orleans. Two Cutters were already there being used for Patrols along the Southern Atlantic region.

He was alerted by two different factions. The Coast Guard contacted him the morning after arrival at the Naval Station and alerted that the Cutter being sent to him would be delayed for three days, but to wait. Second call came from General William Donovan's aide asking him to travel upstream on the Mississippi to squelch rumors that German U-Boats were present or even if any evidence showed up.

This worked out well for him. He had no desire to sit around and wait. He contacted the Base Commander of the call from the Coast Guard and ask his permission (even though he didn't need it) to be gone for a couple of days. Permission was granted. On his way back to his room, he spoke with an enlisted man about where he could rent a vehicle for two days. The Seaman told him of a man in Nutbush, Tennessee, that owned a small used car lot and a small farm. Man's name was Daniel Kelly and Billy Ray learned later he was from Lauderdale County, Alabama.

They hit off at first handshake. He had an old Ford that was great on gas and bad on oil, so the deal was he could rent it but he'd need to buy a case of oil and take it with him. Billy Ray also made a deal with him that upon returning, he'd need to rent a horse and saddle for one day. Deal was struck and after stopping at the hardware store for some camping supplies and case of oil he took off for New Madrid, Missouri to start a scan of the river. His ever- present binoculars at his side and some hearty fried chicken, lemonade and biscuits, he picked up from the local diner, gave him what he needed to begin his scanning.

Twenty- two miles later and stopping about twenty times he drove along the bank and dike of the easterly side of the river and going north, didn't reveal anything. He spent the night under an abandoned gas station's shed. Nice fire under an autumn sky was just right. He was always true to writing in his journal and tonight wasn't an exception.

Next morning, he crossed over to the westerly side and began going south. Oil was pouring through the motor too fast from the Ford. Coming up on a "shade tree" mechanic was what he wanted to find, smoke was billowing from the convertible. He did in fact find one about a mile later. The mechanic heard him before he saw him and was waiting. Billy Ray smiled and asked "Rekon you could find out what my problem is?" Mechanic in his coveralls answered "Don't know what your problem is, but this heah Ford has a bad oil pan and probably gasket. "Then let me ask you, do you have an oil pan and gaskets?" Mechanic just turned around and went inside of the old barn. After about fifteen minutes he returned with a used oil pan and a box assumed to be gaskets. He didn't say anything but jacked the car up and crawled under and went to work.

Meanwhile, Billy Ray walked across the road and made it to the dike. After climbing up, he bent over to tie his shoe when he noticed a rope, like a trot line running in the water. Strange he thought that is dangerous to do that. The more he looked at it, the more he wanted to know. He walked back to his car and retrieved the binoculars and returned to where he'd been standing. Looking across the river he located on the other side where the rope came out of the water. He then went to the water-edge on his side and pulled the rope up but didn't get very far. Now he must find out from the mechanic what all of this means.

Approaching his car, he immediately noticed the car was off the jacks. Mechanic came out with his hands in a rag drying off and said" Took oil from your backseat to reload. Had a hole in your pan and the gaskets had shifted 'cause the pan had shifted.

You okay now." Billy Ray pawed the ground and asked "What do I owe you?" Mechanic answered, "Two dollars for gaskets, three dollars for the oil pan, it was used but no holes, and five dollars for labor."
Billy Ray said ,"Fair enough" as he handed him a ten- dollar bill. "By the way what's your name?" Mechanic put the money in his pocket and answered "Why, are you the law?" Looking him over a little more closely he answered "No, hey, by the way what's the deal with that rope across the river?"

Mechanic answered "Name is Robert Blackburn, Reason for rope, a bunch of my buddies was down here one night and we were just sitting around, when we saw a strange thang in the middle of big muddy. Flashed some light on it and it started backing up. They said it was one of them old boats that stay under water. We got some old tennis court nets from Mr. Wesson' plantation, tied them to some baling wire and barge rope, jumped in my boat and went across stream and tied it to a pole we drove in the ground. Didn't want that thang getting steam and attack somebody."

Billy Ray mentioned how glad he did the right thing, but next time alert the Naval station. He drove on down trying to get a glimpse of any other clues. He crossed over from Arkansas to Nutbush and drove in Mr. Kelly's lot without any smoke coming out and the motor running smoothly. Kelly's demeanor was friendly and open. Billy Ray told him what had been done and asked the profane question to any used car salesman, "Would you sell it?"
"Yes, if the price is right."
"Describe right price"
"500 dollars" "300 dollars" "400 dollars" "350 and that's my last offer"
"Okay, let me get the papers"
"Hold on, gotta go and get some cash."
"Okay"

Billy Ray drove back to port and went in to the small bank there. Money was sent from his bank back in Tuscumbia, Alabama plus a little extra to this bank.

He returned to Mr. Kelley's place and paid him. Leaving his car there, took the black and white pinto with black saddle and returned to where he'd seen the "rope". Leaving a landmark, he looked at the rope placement and could see the tennis nets. Robert Blackburn had been accurate and he'd convinced Billy Ray.

Billy Ray convinced Robert to go to Mr. Kelley's, pick up his car, bring it back to his place and replace clutch and power pressure, change out all belts, put in a new battery, tires and tubes, take into Memphis for new paint job and convertible top. Take it to Naval Station and leave it. Banker at the port bank would take care of all charges including what he charges for labor and all the city travel. Money was transferred to the banker with instruction to trust Robert Blackburn. Upon completion of all tasks, the car was to be parked at the bank.

CHAPTER

TWENTY-FIVE

Before they shoved off to "hunt" German submarines (aka as U-Boats), an event occurred that became a life changer for Billy Ray. The cutter captain was relieved of command, arrested and removed from the decks. Billy Ray was placed as the new commanding officer and cutter captain. He was called in to meet with Admiral Stuart V. Waggoner, at his personal home in Millington. Directed to begin at once and pursue missions in the Gulf of Mexico, just off the shoreline of New Orleans, Admiral Waggoner taught him that NOW wasn't to be treated as YESTERDAY when it came to being a part of these new events. He didn't care if the crew never polished shoes, but were required to polish weapons. Nor did he care that a belt buckle had no shine. He did want the eating utensils clean though. Explanation was straight forward and to the point. Just do your job, care for your crew, destroy enemy, save civilian lives, and stay away from booze. No mistake about intentions. No mistake about request made.

Back on the cutter, he tailed in the officers and the Chief Petty Officer, Huey Walker for the initial staff meeting. Surprised by their reaction when he explained that he was now the captain, which was elation. He began his statements.

Using a facial expression of being a leader, at least that's what Billy Ray imagined, he studied the men present. (They were still tied down in Millington, Tennessee, just north of Memphis), then he began:

"Gentlemen, I'm Lieutenant Billy Ray Coleman. I'm from Tuscumbia, Alabama, but to be more exact, from a river community named "Pride's Landing. I grew up on the Tennessee river. Trained to captain this cutter while attending and graduating from the Academy in New London and special training recently at Cape May. Have already served in combat. This is all you need to know about me now. At this meeting, I want to know more about you. When I point in your direction I'll want to know your name, rank, hometown and state and above all your job description and what you do on our cutter".

He first pointed at the oldest officer, a seemingly thirty-something and if nothing else impressive, both arms held tattoos.

"Sir my name is Ensign Buddy Barnes, I've received a direct officer's rank from Admiral Waggoner due to my experience and training with weapons, especially firing depth charges. I'm from Bad Axe, Michigan. I'm experienced at training how to train our crew on how to fire, maintain, load and gauge, on how to keep us "firing ready ", twenty-four seven. The Chief and I have selected and are in the process of training our crew. We believe and we hope you will feel the same way that majority of our crew should know how to efficient at arms when called upon. This means all weapons and depth charges."

"Thank you and congratulations on your promotion. We'll talk some more later."

He next pointed at the smallest man.

"Sir I am Ensign Bobby Gene Bradford, from Akron, Ohio. I am the Medical Officer. It's permissible to call me "Doc", went to medical school at Johns Hopkins."

Billy Ray didn't at first didn't grasp this man's personality then in the event read him as some type of "yankee" smart aleck, he'd need to establish who was the boss. "I shall refer you as Doctor. If my information is correct, and I'm referring to my notes, orders, and your inventory of medical supplies, I'm wanting you to double your inventory of supplies when we dock in New Orleans. Understand?"

"Sir" asked the Doctor now bewildered, "why"

"Doctor you'll also need to recruit an aide. I'll pay them out of cutter's safe in addition to their regular pay." He was ignoring him for the sake of the Doctor to eat some "humble pie". Looking at the man's eyes and expression as well as the other men present, he knew it was time to explain their orders.

"Men we are headed for war in our own waters. Once we load up and reload, it's the Gulf of Mexico for this cutter. Object is to locate enemy U-Boats and to destroy them. Protect civilian ships. Provide medical treatment to all. Escort whomever we are directed to accommodate.

Training our crew in-route will be imperative. Especially being accurate in usage of depth Charges. Mr. O'Kelly, our expert in sonar, will lead us in this endeavor."

It became quiet in the stateroom until Chief spoke up. "Sir, some questions please?"

"Of course-proceed"

"What about day-to-day activities?"

"You will be in -charge of them. Officer's will be arranging offense and defense plans. They will notify you when any need comes up. Executive Officer O'Kelly will be bridge commander. Chief will be your go -to officer in most events. He will get his orders from me."

"Will we be taking on more crew members?"

"Probably, have asked for trained medical personnel. Asked for another cook that will specialize in nutritional foods. He is to meet us in New Orleans with extra food. We'll need to on-load another freezer to hold meats and will be furnishing us with ice. Medical personnel will need ice also. Need at least two more armament men. Need trained ammo loaders, but will need to reach in our existing personnel for this. Men I know all of this is an anomaly to most of you, but you must adapt without questioning our motives. "

"Sir, I am Ensign Percy Ray, guess I'm OIC for remaining jobs. Food, Human resources, Sewage, etc. will be under my leadership, but let's face it, Chief Walker has forgotten more than I can learn and he runs it excellent. Thought I'll be available for the Chief at any time, but would like to learn weapon firing when we begin training"

"Thank you, Ensign, and will keep your request in consideration."

Chief said, "will work with him sir."

"Okay men, I shall speak one-on-one with each of you while we travel and train. Now Mr. O'Kelly, Chief and the rest of you, let's shove off."

CHAPTER
TWENTY-SIX

Training started immediately as the respective section officers collected their enlisted men who performed assigned tasks like team members should. Maneuvers on the Mississippi river were not the same as they would be on the Gulf, but repetitious movement as to firing of weapons and charges were beneficial.

Upon arrival in New Orleans, each section loaded necessary items that would keep them afloat for at least a month. Ammunition and petrol for duration of how many battles they would be forced to participate in. O'Kelly's sonar and radar were working to perfection, thereby giving members a sense of security. Knowing where the enemy was, gave them a leap forward in battle.

Billy Ray settled in and continued re-learning map reading and making plots. O'Kelly was a great help and was fast becoming a friend that he knew he could depend on. Chief Walker's experience and people skills kept the co-ordination of people and cutter on the same track. The big burly leader just didn't play- around and the crew knew it. At six feet three-inches, and about two hundred forty pounds, respect was given to him without any trouble.

At twenty-three thirty hours on the second night out, all hell broke loose. O'Kelly gave the attack alarm and the crew began moving in fast motion and assumed positions for necessary attacks or rafts to save individuals. The passenger ship, ROBERT E. LEE, was hit by one torpedo from the enemy U-Boat 166 at about fifty miles from New Orleans. It sunk in fifteen minutes. However, many survived and Billy Ray's rafts loaded up thirty-two of them. Sadly, over one hundred perished. The escortship that was unable to halt the initial attack by using depth charges sunk the U-Boat 166, and were successful to pull many survivors from the sea.

With the fury of a pack of wolves, the mighty crew were determined to sink some enemy U-Boats and anything the Nazi-navy put in their way. At first many hours of nothing, but the further out to sea they went, more activity began to pop up on the sonar screen.

Torpedoes were dropped when the alert system made them aware of "harm's way". Immediate impact was made and their first "sinking" brought cheers from the men and staff. Billy Ray was happy to send the proper information and the coordinates of the strike. But not to tarry, they again went back on the hunt and this time they were successful using depth charges.

They took the survivors to Venice, Louisiana for medical treatment and re-fueling. From there, Billy Ray made his first telephone call to Heidi. She answered the call instead of "Sissy".

"Hallo, this is Heidi"

"Hi Heidi, this is Billy Ray, how are you doing? "Billy Ray, are you calling from the war?" "Kinda, but are you okay?"

"Ya Billy Ray, but I miss you. When you coming home?" "Miss you too. Don't know when I'll get back.

"Love America. Thank you for saving me. Have not heard anything from my family. Mr. Bud Goodloe is trying to find them."

"If anyone can, Bud will do it."

"Billy Ray when I see you again, I'm going to kiss you." (laughter)

"That will be just fine Heidi" (laughter) "You want to speak with Sissy?"

"Yes, and Heidi, I'll send you letters soon." Sissy got on the line.

"Hello Billy Ray, how are you?"

"Great, can't tell you where I am or when I'll come home but would love to see ya'll and Pride's Landing."

"What you mean is you would love to see Heidi; right?" "That too."

"You've made her day. You are all she talks about. Thanks for calling. I'll let you speak to Heidi before your time is up."

"Hallo again Billy Ray. Come home soon. I want to see you bad."

"I'll try hard to get some time to come home and see you. Glad you like America. Bye Bye."

"Bye Billy Ray, think I love you."

They hung up telephones, but her last remark thrilled him immensely.

ATTACKING AGAIN

Upon refueling, they headed back to sea and the battles. This time they were directed to browse the coastlines from Louisiana and now near Mississippi, Alabama, Georgia and a small area near Beaufort, South Carolina. Along these routes special attention was made during the dark hours to inspect the beaches for any inhabitants. Even the Chief couldn't ascertain this importance, but so far, all that Billy Ray did was satisfactory to him. They had been at sea for two months when one evening one of his observers noticed convoluted folks running up and down the beach and digging in the areas between the sand dunes. They seemingly were shouting to each other.

Billy Ray was awaken and he went topside to observe what was happening. As soon as he focused in with the powerful spy glass, he just knew they were Nazis and called his shore patrol topside to invade the beach and capture them. He spent about fifteen minutes talking to his OIC and Petty Officer who would be leading the skiffs that would be going ashore. Sails only, one-hundred per-cent capture, and very little firearm display were part of the orders. Dressed in Navy-blue tunics and trousers with black boots, skull cap and black camouflage for their exposed flesh. They men armed themselves with small machine guns, .45 pistols and one grenade. One medic was sent with them in the event of injury to anyone.

At midnight, they slipped from the mother cutter and sailed silent in an easterly formation. After losing sight of the people, on the beach, they turned north to the beachhead and went ashore for the capture. Pulled the two skiffs on shore and secured the anchor. Crawling and trotting in a bent formation back toward the groups assembled, Ensign James Gamble, OIC, directed the shore patrol to spread in two-man formation but the medic and radioman to stay close to him.

Gamble had studied German while attending college at Cornell and was selected to be on this sea-craft per request from the "skipper". In addition, he seemed to be a fearless leader. These were the reasons Billy Ray selected him to take this very adventurous mission. To codify it, hand signals were assigned. The "skipper" taught Gamble which one to use. Seems that he'd used them before. In any event this is what they did.

Silently they approached and quickly surrounded the men huddled in the area between two large sand dunes.

"Halt" exclaimed Gamble, "Hande hoch" (hands up). This they did. The shore patrol moved in and using their flashlights, placed beams on the captured. "Legan nach unten" (lay down). Again, they complied. "American erfassen" (you've being captured by Americans) "dos suche (search). Gamble's men came forward and did an arm's inspection on the Nazi. Clearing the threat by removing all pocket items including pocket knives. They then stood them up and placed rope manacles on them.

Kommen sie mit, (come with me) ordered Gamble and led them to where the two skiffs were located. Counting all that had been captured, they would be overloaded but using his radio, he called in to have the cutter to head to them with lights on. The faster the cutter found them the less danger they'd be in.

As they were loading, one of the captive introduced himself in English: "Sir my name is Gobles, commander of a U-Boat that ran aground. We evacuated and swam to where you found us. My compliments on your capture. You caught us without making a sound. Not to worry sir, we are glad to be in your hands. We will not cause any trouble. May I ask what branch of the military you represent?"

"Coast Guard".

"Are you and your people local?"

"Nein, how come you speak English so well?" "Studied in England"

They boarded the skiffs and sailed to the mother cutter, which was already heading their way. Gobles explained to his men they were in good hands and would be sent, he thought, to a prisoner of war camp, so, in all probability, would be out of the war. His men smiled broadly and thanked the Coast Guardsmen who gave them blankets and cigarettes. Once they reloaded on the cutter, were given dry clothing and ham sandwiches/coffee. The chief put them in the brig and they made their way to Savannah, Georgia for placement of the

Captives. Gobles was sent for interview with Billy Ray with Gamble as interpreter.

CHAPTER
TWENTY-SEVEN

Upon arrival in Savannah, Georgia, Billy Ray secured much needed three-day passes for his crew. He spent a day doing reports to both Coast Guard and the O.SS. He then took some time off and toured Savannah. Alone and lonely, anguish took over at times. He still missed Gloria, but in his heart, he knew that was over. She'd married and after all this time, if she still wanted him, she'd made arrangement to find him.

Heidi on the over hand wrote him daily and never failed to tell him how much she missed him. He walked around just trying to see any female that reminded him of her. He couldn't take it any longer, so he telephoned her and even if they spoke for only a few minutes, he sensed from the sound of her voice she was sincere in telling him how she felt. He never found anyone that looked or sounded like Heidi. He told himself he just had to see and hold her.

The shore patrol located him as he left a high-school football game.

"Sir would you be in the Coast Guard?" A navy petty-officer asked him.

"Depends on who wants to know."

"Port commander wants us to deliver Lieutenant Billy Ray Coleman. Are you that person?"

"Yes. Do you require ID?"

"Yes sir"

Billy Ray displayed proper information and then got in the Plymouth. He was taken to an office near the southern square park and dropped off. Directions were given to him on how to locate the Port Commander. He knocked on the second-floor walnut door with the name:

Commander Lee Crittenden, USCG. Port Commander. Deep bass voice said "enter". Billy Ray opened the door took two strides to an antique desk, popped to attention, saluted and exclaimed "Sir, Lieutenant Billy Ray Coleman reporting as ordered."

Salute from the Commander was returned and he said, "have a seat Lieutenant".

"What may I do for the Commander explained Billy Ray"

"It's this way Coleman, you are to take your cutter back north out of New Orleans. Your replacement will take over in Memphis and will return to Alaska. You will contact your HQ in Washington for further orders once you arrive at Millington. Your crew will he replaced in New Orleans, and your replacements crew will take over operations. You will captain until you arrive in Memphis. Shove off 0600 hours."

"Sir question if I may?"

"Certainly"

"What about my men?"

"They will be reassigned to other cutters in this area. Possibility of replacement cutter arriving and they will be assigned to her."

"Thank you, sir, I'll prepare for my journey'

He immediately went back to the cutter and after locating Chief Jackson, he passed on the information about the recent events.

Finishing the captain's log which he learned the first day of their missions, became so historical that for the first time in his life he was so proud of the many endeavors he and the crew undertook, gave him a lot of pride.

The Chief assembling the crew together, learned the officers were very saddened about the change. After all they said for over three months they had been in sustained combat situations and had sunk five U-boats, captured a crew from a sunk sea craft and a U-boat and saved thirty -two survivors of the ROBERT E. LEE. The leadership of Lieutenant Billy Ray Coleman, had been outstanding and all aboard had great respect and affection for him.

Meanwhile, dressed for cruising up the Mississippi river, Billy Ray also felt sadness for the loss of the cutter and the breaking-up of this excellent crew. He sent out to the files of them, letters of commendation and recommendations of promotion and ribbons. He addressed them with mention of thanks and admiration. Tears formed in his eyes as he shook each man's hand and told them goodbye.

"Request permission to come aboard" he asked the new captain.

"Request granted, welcome back"

Billy Ray came aboard and was greeted by Lieutenant Howard Smith Edwards, the expert in "Ice" maneuvers. This cutter was so geared and built for Alaska, that it was very much needed to go "back home." A new cutter that the Coast Guard had purchased from the Navy, was in process of being rebuilt for combat situations. This was the replacement that hopefully would re-crew his former staff.

CHAPTER
TWENTY-EIGHT

Knowledgeable that no new mission awaits him from the Coast Guard and the O.S.S and questioning himself should he leave at once to see Heidi, he decided to remain in Millington and check out the mission he didn't complete about the U-boat submerged going upstream on the Mississipi river.

He went to his bank and transferred funs back to his bank in Tuscumbia, just keeping enough for a few days and traveling money. While at the bank, he collected his ford convertible that had been upgraded and paid for from his funds at the bank. Banker told him that his investment had made him a very comfortable amount of money.

Next morning, he drove to the farm that housed his pinto---"Domino" and saddle/tact. While coming into contact with his animal, he saw his old friend Pete, from whom he'd bought the horse. "Hey Pete! how you doing?"

"Great sir, glad to see you again."

"Just got back from the gulf, and headed back to Alabama. Picked up my car and wanted to see about getting the horse sent back to a stable at home. Need your phone number so I can call you where you can bring Domino to me or can I hire you to do that for me?"

"Yeah, just let me know when and where"

"Will do, probably in a month."

"Sir, been curious about that boat sunk in "Big Muddy", did you ever find it?

"Nope but think I'd like to take Domino and go upstream and

search some more for a couple days."

"How about tomorrow morning at 8:00, if I could leave my car here.

"Sure, will have him ready, but you better get some camping stuff if you are going to be gone overnight. Go down to hardware store and get a big 'ol bag and rope. Shoot if'n I wasn't so busy here I'd like to go with you if it would be okay."

"Hey would love to have you go with me if you had your own horse."

"Well, will see, but anyhow I'll have yo hoss ready."

Billy Ray left and went down to hardware store and grocery and bought what he'd need. Bought a .38 and ammo also, never could be too careful.

Next morning showed up on time wearing jeansm flannel shirt, cowboy boots, jacket and straw cowboy hat. To his surprise, Pete was ready with an old brown sway-back and pulling a mule loaded with a tent.

They left and rode on the east bank checking out anything agape. They made it up to the area where Robert Blackburn's shop was on the west side and pitched their camp. This was where he had been told that a U-boat had sunk and the crew left the area walking. Just a rumor but he wanted to check it out for a couple of days.

That night, the stars was beaming and it gave Pete and him an opportunity to get better vision. Found nothing but the next morning took a piece of plywood and floated around. Once they tired out and went back to the campsite, two men were sitting down building a fire. Neither Pete nor Billy Ray knew them but greeted, nonetheless.

The older fellow returned the acknowledgment and asked, "Whatcha boys doin'?"
Billy Ray answered, "Trying to find a submerged boat."
"What for"
"I'm in the Coast Guard and my boss wants me to look around them as scrap iron down in Memphis."
"I'll say, it was something. Folks say funny stuff about junk

in the river. If you find anything else, turn it in to the Coast Guard in Millington. Probably give you more than scrapyard.

"Do tell"

"Yessir"

"Well, what if I found out about people that sailed here?"

"Contact officer in charge of the Coast Guard and they will contact me, I'm moving on to other mission."

Billy Ray and Pete looked around some more and then headed back to the farm, fed animals and loaded equipment in back seat of the Ford.

Next morning Billy Ray decided to go home to Pride's Landing and to Heidi. He decoded she was the right person for him and he loved her.

CHAPTER

TWENTY-NINE

Leaving Memphis in the convertible in the afternoon headed east toward Alabama, gave him a sense of euphoria. He was smiling broadly because after many letters and a few telephone calls, he was getting to see her—Heidi. The thoughts of Gloria were fading but he did desire to know if she was all right. Aw well, he was sure someone back home would tell him. For now, the proverbial girl he left behind, was about to leave the dream world and become reality.

Within an hour, he topped a hill and drove into the quaint railroad city of Corinth, Mississippi. Finding a men's clothing store wasn't hard nor was finding the clothing and his size either. He hadn't worn civilian clothing in a while and was excited at the possibility. Especially wearing new shoes.

Not far out of town he located a "PURE" petrol truck stop that contained showers and a restaurant. For twenty-five cents for the warm shower and for a dollar and fifty cents, a meal made for "the gods". He needed them both. Wearing his new clothing and shoes, for a minute, in his revere, he was back in Deshler High School. Only fifty miles to go excited him more.

A short hour passed and once he came upon Cherokee, Alabama, he started looking for the unpaved road leading to his home, Pride's Landing.

It was still light, with the moon on the horizon though, he turned and saw the home that John Pride had built. Now it contained her. He pulled in the driveway and parked at the side of the house. As he got out of the car, stood and stretched, he immediately smelled the many aromas coming up from the Tennessee river. Now he knew for certain he was home.

Stepping up the steps to the porch, he didn't realize how much anxiety he felt, and it enhanced as he looked through the crack of the front door that was ajar and saw her sitting at the kitchen table eating her evening meal. Now he wanted to thrill and surprise her. Sneaking in, tip-toeing, and moving slowly, he came up on her backside. She dropped her fork, turned with large eyes and screamed "BILLLLLY---RAYYYY', YOU ARE HOME. With that, she jumped up and began hugging him. The hug turned into a kiss while the normal demure SISSY, just sat there with big eyes, mouth opened as wide as possible, and mashed potatoes drooling down the side of her gorgeous lips.
Love was in the air!!!

CHAPTER

THIRTY

For The remainder of the evening, Billy Ray and Heidi sat on the porch swing, holding hands, kissing and just falling more in love. When the fatigue from all his events finally took over, he went to sleep on the sofa in the living room.

In the morning, he was awaken imaginable by a brush kiss and a hot cup of coffee. When he opened his eyes, he looked in the most beautiful blue eyes imaginal.liebe dich" she murmured, "guten morgan"

"Sugar, I told you last night, I don't speak German. Talk to me in English until you teach me your language."

She loved for him to call her Sugar, he just didn't know it yet.
In her coquetry state of mind, she continued using her language. "Wie gehts dir?"

He couldn't help but grin and said "I know that one and the answer is now that I'm with you, I'm fine."

Again, "was machst du heute?" "What"

"What are going to do today is what I'm asking."

"Spend it with you" he said while sipping his coffee."

"Liber, ich liebe dich! ! !"

"Me too, know that one also."

He stood up and they embraced. "Gotta shave and take a shower."

She then smiled and spoke English, "How do you want your eggs?"

"Scrambled, but wait for a while, I'll be in the bathroom preparing myself for you. With that, he got out of his suitcase the items and clothing he'd need.

After breakfast, he took her for a spin in the convertible. She didn't know how to drive but was silent and observed his moves as he drove. Some day she thought "I'll learn to drive and this will be my car too. He doesn't know it yet, but I plan to marry him."

Instead of just a spin, they did the popular riding around type of date. Sissy had left "Pride's Landing" to spend sonic time with her brother's wife Jane, that was home for a while. Her husband was serving on the staff of the Governor of Alabama, Frank Dixon, as Adjutant General. They came upon a farm that was housing many horses and other animals. Billy Ray drove up to the farmhouse and blew his horn. A lady that appeared to be in her forties came to the door and stepped on the porch. Dressed in a blue gingham housedress and sporting a very white apron, she asked "why ya'll blowing a horn at us. Didn't anyone ever tell ya'll that was rude."

"Sorry but couldn't tell if ya'll were home. I'm looking for someone to tell me where there is a place that could keep a couple of horses for me while I go back to the Coast Guard. Glad to pay for their upkeep of course and to ride them occasionally. Would you know of such a place?"

"Yes, I do, you can do it here. Price is one hundred dollars per horse, per year. My folks will come over each Sunday and ride them. When will you want to deliver?"

"Not sure yet. One is in Memphis and I'll have to send for him. Will buy, I hope, another one this week. Will have saddles and tack for them also."

He stepped out of the car and wrote a check for the feed and handling.

"Oh! I remember you, you live down at "Pride's Landing" with the Goodloe family. She was smiling now. Guess you know we are the Bigbee family."

"Yes imam I do. This makes me feel better 'cause ya'll have a great reputation for taking care of horses."

"Thank you so, 'predate you being so forthright. We'll take care of your horses. Bye now, got to go back and take my beans from the stove."

"Bye 'mam.:"

They drove on in to Tuscumbia, and went to the new restaurant, named the "B & W" and enjoyed steaks broiled to perfection. Heidi

108

couldn't figure out why wine wasn't served. He explained to her the laws about partaking of alcohol in this county, she just rolled her eyes.

They walked around town, holding hands as lovers do, until they saw the marque at the "Strand" movie house. In big bold letters, it said 'RAZOR's Edge'. He'd heard about this new movie and decided to take her to see it and to learn a little about the old south.

Three hours later, they reappeared from the theatre, and once he got to see her eyes again, he noticed they had changed. Of course, they were still sky blue, but now they cast a look of total love and dreamy. In front of the people walking out of the theatre, he kissed her. Then he took her by hand and led her back to the car, opened the door for her, and kissed her again. Once they were inside, she snuggled up to him. He then drove north for a few blocks and entered the gate to Miss Helen Keller's house and parked near the cypress tree that he and Gloria had shared many hours under. Undertaking the next two steps of understanding, were extremely hard for him. Number one was explaining all about Gloria to her and number two, asking her to marry him. To the first step, she listened patiently, because she had already been told about Gloria. The second step, she said "YESSSS". He then took her back "Pride's Landing."

On Sunday, after Jane returned, they took the short drive to luka, Mississippi, where they were wed. During those days, the marriage laws were more liberal in Mississippi, so for a quick marriage, folks from all over came there for their vows and license. Going back, Jane and Sissy sang the old civil war song, "the Rose of Alabama." They kept singing as they got in Jane's car and left "Pride's Landing."

Billy Ray and Heidi, had a wonderful and blissful wedding night.

CHAPTER

THIRTY-ONE

Before daylight, Billy Ray headed out on highway seventy- two going east toward the small community named Courtland. It had been a headquarters for the Alabama Calvary during the civil war. It was also the home of General Joe Wheeler, their leader. Now it housed an Army Air Corp training facility. It also was where General Bill Donovan of the O.S.S., was going to meet him.

Upon arriving at the guarded gate, the non-commissioned-officer in charge, was a man that Billy Ray met in New Orleans, by the name of Quincy du Bois, a full fledge Cajun that also had been an alligator hunter. In his Cajun dialect, after recognizing Billy Ray he said "Hey tis you my frand, member you well. I guarded yo coast guard, ship-boat. Yo a big man. Whatcha doing heah wearing people clothes stead of sailor-boy suit?"

"Gotta meet a man my friend. Name is Billy Ray Coleman, by the way. Check your list and see if my name is on it."

After checking he said, "as shore as my name came from my Pappy, it tis. You ain't got no twice-barrel shotgun on you, do you? Shore need one, 'dem duck fly ovah heah all the time. Cookie said he'd fix 'urn up iffen I coughd scarf up some fat 'uns."

"No Corporal, no shotguns or any other weapons." "Well sign heah and go on in and do yo bzness."

Billy Ray drove on in and located the administration office and walked in to report his presence. A PFC asked him to have a seat in the outer office and wait for a ride. He was going to be taken to the DC-10

110

waiting on the tarmac. The PFC, was curious why a person wearing a plaid shirt, blue-jeans, and cowboy boots, was receiving such preferred treatment.

He went up the ladder of the plane and there waiting was General Donovan. He was a striking man in a royal blue suit, white shirt, blue tie, perfectly shined black shoes. His startling appearance spoke at once with his shiny grey hair and tanned face. No smiles, no "happy to see you" attitude. Just business.

"Coleman, here is your assignment. You are to proceed to Europe to learn how to train troops in special hand-to-hand combat, tactics, and survival missions. Two special people namely Major Paddy Mayne of Great Britain and Colonel Viktor Leonov of Russia, will be your instructors. You'll leave out of Cuba on a sugar cane merchant ship, headed for Spain. From there, the French/German underground will take you to Northern France where you will fly an aeronca 11 chief single Engine to southern Finland, where you'll bail out and allow the plane to crash. The Russians will collect you for instruction. After your training with the Russians, which will be about a month, you'll take another plane or proceed on a ship to England where you'll team up with Payne who will specialize in ordinance and heavy weapons. This will take about a month there also. I'll then contact you for further orders. I'll tell you this!! A new Brigade that merges Americans and Canadians for a special assignment will be under your command. Even the top officers will be under your guidance. Lord Mountbatten, is the "daddy rabbit" for this endeavor. As a matter of fact, they are paying your expenses.

You are to report each day of this week, including today, here, to learn how to fly. You know how to para-jump, but if you need more time to practice, do it here. In addition, you must learn how to speak as much German as possible. You'll need to leave next Sunday and arrange your own travel means from here to Key West, Florida to meet with Mr. Ernest Hemingway, who will transport you to Cuba for loading up on the "sugar" ship to Spain. By the way, go and retrieve your enigma and give it back to me now. Your written orders and money will be given to you when you return.

Billy Ray did as he was told and within ten minutes he returned with the valued communication instrument.
As the prepared to make their farewell handshake, Billy Ray then asked'

Sir, one question, did I understand you correctly when you said Ernest Hemingway?'

"Yes, the writer, and for your information he is a KGB agent."

"Well thanks for clearing that up for me"

'uh-- -uhi Coleman, congratulations on your wedding. She can teach you how to speak her language"

"But how did you know?"

The door closed in his face as the big twin engines fired up. Billy Ray reported to the instructor assigned to him, Lieutenant Mark Tomlin, who began the intense flow of learning.

Instruments on the Piper Cub he would be assigned to was first. He was drilled and then graded. He passed easily. Tomorrow he would begin to start the plane and drive it around. This would be a chance to use the instruments.

As he was departing through the gates, Corporal du Bois, was getting in his jeep. They waived and Billy Ray, remembering he had an old Springfield 1903 rifle and ammunition back at "Pride's Landing" and made a mental note to load it up and present it to du Bois in the morning. He drove the thirty something miles home to his bride. Excited and full of desire.

CHAPTER
THIRTY-TWO

In the morning of departure for Europe/war, he took a quick cruise on his skiff. Upon arriving at the dock, he walked back to "Pride's Landing." At the top of the hill, he knelt at the Prayer Rock for a long but in-depth prayer. He arose with tears in his eyes and walked to the front porch where waiting for him with a smile on her face stood his darling wife. She was driving him to Tuscumbia to catch the train to Chattanooga. From there he would catch a greyhound for Miami and then another train to Key West. A long arduous trip for at least three days.

He would be wearing dungarees, hard-toed boots, chambray shirt and a Navy pea-coat. He'd grown a pencil-thin moustache and had allowed his hair to grow longer.

He'd meet Ernest Hemingway in Key West who would take him to Cuba to board ship toward Lisbon, Portugal. From there he was suppose to fly to Finland.

He was thinking as they drove to the train station that he'd taught Heidi how to drive and she had taught him Yiddish and German. They arrived on time, embraced and kissed. He put an envelope filled with cash into her purse, got out threw his duffle bag over his shoulder and boarded the train. She waved at him after he selected assigned seat and waved at her. The train jerked and she went back to her car and drove away but only after making a couple of blocks, she stopped pulled over and the wept extensively.

He was thinking as they drove to the train station that he'd taught Heidi how to drive and she had taught him Yiddish and German. They arrived on time, embraced and kissed. He put an envelope filled with cash into her purse, got out threw his duffle bag over his shoulder and boarded the train. She waved at him after he selected assigned seat and waved at her. The train jerked and she went back to her car and drove away but only after making a couple of blocks, she stopped pulled over and the wept extensively.

Billy Ray got a blanket and pillow from the overhead, put the pillow over his face and for the second time today wept. Later he reminisced about the first time he left to join the military service, he wept then but for losing Gloria. Now he felt nothing else for her. He missed those guys he went for boot camp then. He wondered about them more and more and prayed for them. He prayed for the guys he'd been with on the Gulf of Mexico too.

That afternoon, he caught his greyhound for Miami. Picking some how to learn to speak Spanish language books to help alter language barrier was a must.

He had to linger for a day before he caught the train for key West and insert in the war again.

CHAPTER

THIRTY-THREE

The two men, almost identical in size and looks, eyed and scanned each other like gunslingers from the "old west". Each had mustaches the same color and size and they twitched them the same way. Hemingway was dressed in an old button-up type shirt that at one time had been white. Now with the almost constant sweating and sand grime, it was a putrid yellow. His trousers were as if he'd never taken them off.
Rolled up at each cuff, faded blue cotton-type. A red bandanna circled his neck and coupled with the hemp made sandals, gave the appearance of a beach-bum.
Billy Ray, however, was neater in appearance. Seaman look to be exact. Denim shirt and trousers, hard -toed black naval boots, and the white sailor cap, made him available for perceived no-good, bar fighting "toughie". Except for the under-stated white scarf that his wife had given to him as he packed for an extended stay in parts of the world he had never dreamed he'd visit. Only difference was he displayed a twinkle in his eyes that said, "I'm not afraid of you and you don't intimidate me at all. But I am curious about you"

"Well stranger, what'll you drink, I'm buying". Said Hemingway.

"Just a glass of ice-tea if it's available." answered Billy Ray.

"Where you from? From the sound of your accent, I'd guess in the south."

"Kinda, just travel around a bit. Bet you and I know some of the same people.

"Like who?"

"Wild Bill Donovan"

"Yep, he and me went quail huntin' once. I bagged more and it

115

irked him" he said with a laugh.

"Is there any place we can talk without so many people listening?"

Billy Ray got his ice-tea and started looking around "Sloppy Joe's". He began looking just outside the door and noticing some small tables and chairs, which Billy Ray figured would be a good place for them to be alone for their meeting, pointed Hemingway picked up on the eye-search and head beckoned Billy Ray to follow him as they went outside. Upon sitting down, Ernest Hemingway began his self-taught manner of character "ripping". "Well young man you know Bill Donovan, so what?"

"He sent me to find you." "Why?"

"To aid me in arranging passage on a Cuban ship destined for Portugal."

"Well, who are you?"

"Code name is Danny Driscoll. Look Mr. Hemingway, I don't play games with people. My job is to finish what I start. I'm on an assignment and it will be done. If you are trying to intimidate me, then you are "barkin' up the wrong tree."

"You need to be taken down a peg or two. I'm a KGB agent for the U.S.S.R., I've taken down U-Boats, and shot off antennas on many therefore taking them out of service. So, don't try to bully me either." Said Hemingway

"I have read your file sir, and you have my respect and am an avid fan of your writings. We are on the same side and in my zeal, I might come across as blustery, and I apologize for that but my time is very important and I do seek and appreciate any help you can give me." Retorted BIlly Roy.

"Well said and I shall cooperate with you. Tell you what, go inside and get yourself a bucket of boiled shrimp and start building up your energy. I've got an errand I must run while you eat. We'll get things in motion and go over to Cuba. That's where I live now By the way, you still need to be taken down the proverbial peg or two", he said with a grin on his face.

"So be it" he answered with like type of grin.

While waiting, Billy Ray heeded the advice given and polished off a small tub of boiled shrimp, some lobster tails and the best clams he'd ever eaten. Many people came over and while friendly, he didn't invite any to join him. Perhaps innocent, but he just couldn't take a chance. Hemingway returned and after drinking a very large container of ale, finally told him that all had been taken care of and they left for Cuba on

Hemingway's fishing boat.

They were still leery of each other and as soon as they cast off, Billy Ray was asked for identification. He had no choice and showed his O.S.S., card and his military card. While they were traveling on the high seas, he kept his back to the cabin wall.

He hadn't trust Hemingway yet to ask him for a hand-gun. He'd do that later. All that Hemingway told him was that he'd be boarding a merchant ship vessel bound for Lisbon, Portugal.

Not that Hemingway was in any way going to turn down the request from General Donovan, but the jealous factor had begun to take over and he wanted to get this over as quick as possible. What the mission was didn't interest him, because he knew it was top secret, but this was all he could be involved in caused him to have the jealousy.

They docked at an area in Cuba that was renown as a hiding place for castaways, criminals, and smugglers known as "Lugar del diablo." He was extracted under cover of darkness and placed on a work crew boarding the Portuguese Merchant ship, "Navegando Para 0 Ce'u" (sailing for heaven). Once on board, he was summoned to Captain's staff headquarters for an introduction to his host for a month sailing. El Captain Lucas Capto, needed a sonar expert. Now that he had been given one by the United States Navy, he easily agreed to take on an American that could set up, maintain and teach one of his men how to operate it for the security and safety it would bring. Captain Capto was an older man and was taken back at the youthfulness of Billy Ray. Joining them with interpretation duties was Mr. Treavor St. Jean, another older man. His erudition was evident just from his stately charm. However, the Captain just didn't impress. But through Mr. St. Jean, Billy Ray learned the Captain was more intelligent than he seemed. He was excellent in games of chance and played chess on the expert level he was told.

Hemingway sped off just as soon as he disposed of Billy Ray and didn't look back. Naturally this brought about a lot of distrust from the young Alabamian, but he wanted more reason than his suspicious and inquired to Mr. St. Jean. The Captain guessed their conversation was about Hemingway and added much dialog to Mr. St. Jean. Before he could answer Billy Ray, ceremony dictated he should answer the older man first. He and the Captain began laughing at something the Captain said. Patiently, Billy Ray just grinned and waited.

"Mousier Coleman, the Captain wanted to apologize for your initial arrival on this vessel. He isn't though respectful of his writings, one of dislike for "El Ernesto". You were dropped off so quickly because Hemingway didn't want to have a confrontation with "El Captain" because he owed him many gambling debts. All parties laughed at that.

HEMMINGWAY'S CARIBBEAN SEA PATROLS

Many tales about Ernest Hemingway were spoken about the Nobel prize recipient during this time. He lived in his home, Finca Vigia, in Cuba when the war began in nineteen thirty -nine. It is said that his first contribution to the Allied war-effort without leaving the island was to organize his own counterintelligence force to root out any Axis sPles operating in Havana. Naming his group "Crook Factory" that was made up of eighteen men including two of his sons and many of his friends from the Spanish civil war. He sought to capture the German spy living in Cuba, Heinz Luning, but those of stronger egos like: Cuban President Batista, General Benitez, J. Edgar

Hoover and even Nelson Rockefeller, took precedent and executed. Hemingway felt left out.

Just three weeks after receiving from Ambassador Braden to form the tongue-in-cheek "Crook Factory", he was also given permission to arm his fishing boat, the Pilar, for patrols against

U-boats off the coast of Cuba. This he did with machine guns, grenades, and his vast array of shotguns and rifles. Many times, he would just patrol around in what seemingly was a pleasure craft or fishing boat, trying to tempt the U-boats to surface and board, and when they did, the boarding party would be disposed of with the machine-gun, and the U-boat disposed of with bazookas and hand grenades. In Naval terms, this was known as the 0-ship-- theory.

Hemingway's patrols against the Nazi U-boats turned out to be just as unsuccessful as the counter-intelligence operation was. As time passed, and only a few U-boats to pursue, the PILAR's patrols turned out to be only fishing trips. More often than naught, the intake of alcohol, would've made their aim inaccurate. A Cuban sailor once said Hemingway was "a playboy that hunted submarines off the Cuban coast as a whim." The Russians, who earlier in China recruited him to serve as an agent in the KGB. Using the name ARGO, he was to keep them informed as well as other allies on the activities of the Nazi, wherever he went, especially in the Caribbean.

Trouble was in his zeal to be important in his leadership of "Crook Factory", he did some detrimental activities that caused the Russians to seek him out and reprimand. Hemingway once told of an episode: "Yesterday afternoon, as the sun was setting, got a little drunk drinking absinthe, thought I saw an antenna of a Nazi-U-boat, shot it off. Expected them to surface and we could take them. Trouble was, it was a comrade from the village of Vyborg, and he was upset. Said he was going to report me. Didn't I realize how costly it was to disperse antennas? Quit shooting at anything on the open seas except gulls.

CHAPTER

THIRTY-FOUR

As the ship was being loaded with bags of sugar and bales of sugar cane, plus petrol and ships stores, Billy Ray locked in the sonar and began the functions. Assigned to him to be the sonar officer and crew were a group of Portugal's finest electronic people. This would be their initial run and all training would be initiated from Billy Ray's documents that he'd posted while serving the Coast Guard in the Gulf of Mexico.

Immediately, upon cast-off, attention to detail began. Billy Ray served as officer-in-charge of sonar for the first twenty -four hours. Training co-existed with his normal duties. As they left the Caribbean Sea and ventured into the Atlantic Ocean, he at last turned the sonar duties over to the Sonar- Officer, Jon Kerru, who exemplified unusual traits.

Catching up on much needed rest and nutritional meals, Billy Ray arose to more energy and strength. Surprisingly, the entire crew and officers treated him with respect and friendliness. He donned Portugal's uniforms and rank and this amplified his stature.

Concern was for potential dangers other than U-boats though. As they floated near the coastlines of Africa, strange vessels with entire population on-board being what seemingly were from the African continent since they were black. Spy glasses reported many cannons and machine guns were manned. Since the Nazi belief did not endorse anyone Negro, they perhaps were Pirates. He passed this on to the Captain, who set up security people and monitors.

In addition, aircraft flew over them periodically without sufficient wing identification. Therefore, with the Captain's permission, he opened the radar boxes that America had sent to Portugal for their many ports. With his assigned crew, they mounted the radar on masts and put them in motion.

Even this wasn't a Q-ship, it behooved them to pull out from the hull, twin forty -millimeter anti-aircraft cannons and assemble them. Ammunition was under the ship storage and were hoisted on deck, camouflaged with the sugar cane bales and prepared to go into action.
The radar revealed that they were being flanked by German aircraft, but eventually flew away. However, the "Pirates" didn't and made an attack on them. Billy Ray and St. Jean got the crew ready and just as the first volley was fired at them, the command was given to return fire. They did and a quick turn-around was initiated and the Africans abandoned the action and fled. Billy Ray directed the return fire and he was proud that they did make a strike.

Truly, he was very important to the "Navegando para O Ce'u" and was decorated by the Captain. Later though, time just lagged, and Billy Ray took this time to prepare for the next weeks by conditioning his body, practicing the oriental martial arts he was being taught by the Korean cooks and firing the nine -millimeter "Lugar," forty-five American pistol, and the Springfield nineteen 0 three rifle. The weapons all belonged to Mr. St. Jean, who he learned had once been an ambassador from France.

The many other men aboard gave indication that they were accomplished knife and sabre fighters and taught him well. He'd taught himself to be proficient with the Native American "Tomahawk" and returned the favors and taught this form of self-protection.
In the evening, the Captain, through Mr. St. Jean, taught him the intracity of Chess. He couldn't wait to return to "Pride's Landing?' and destroy Bud Goodloe. Come to think of it, he wondered if his bride could play? He laughed when he thought, "he'd let her win." Coming into port of Lisbon, he and the crew dismantled the cannons and the radar. The sonar would stay. He knew he'd miss this assemble of merchant marines. They were special to him and all bid him a fond farewell when he signed off the vessel.

CHAPTER

THIRTY-FIVE

Far away from the torrid waves and the bustling city of Lisbon, Billy Ray's thoughts went back to his new wife and the one person he loved above all. He missed her so much which caused him to pursue endeavors he'd never known, like best and quite way to commit murder in combat. During his youth in the orphanage, growing up with very little supervision, and enduring poverty, he dreamed of someone like Heidi. He thought that Gloria was that person, but her lack of fidelity and deep love proved she wasn't.

If he could only see her for just a moment, or read a letter from her, or even see a blurry snapshot; would help him but this conjecture could not be due to his link to the O.S.S.

Meanwhile, back in Alabama, Heidi, along with Mr. Tuthill the architect, Mr. Black the builder and Sissy, all sat around the big kitchen table studying the blueprints of the new home that would be built on the property near the original house built by Mr. Pride in the last century. Big mugs of coffee were being sipped. Even Heidi, who grew up drinking only tea, had converted and become a coffee drinker. The three advisors to

Heidi had convinced her to be more modern in the construction of her home and do away with the dream of "Tara" as in "Gone with the Wind." Their reasoning was that Billy Ray was more conservative and had great taste. She certainly didn't want to do anything that would upset him. Her love was so strong and she missed him terribly. She had a few photographs but her memories displayed a more handsome man and very virile. She couldn't wait until he returned,and they started a family.

Plumbing and electricity was the problem now. Not enough manpower due to most of the young men had been drafted.

However, the charming and beautiful Sissy had a way to solve this problem. She had already contacted her younger brother, Gerald, and directed him to find Reverend Ples and ask him to meet her at her "Pride's Landing." He'd have a solution because his affection for Billy Ray was well known. The previous evening, he and his wonderful wife, Daisy, visited and after ascertaining the needs, told her to instruct the people involved he'd furnish the people.

Among the people sitting at the table with worried looks on their faces, sat Sissy without a frown but rather a smug smile. "Folks she said, not to fret! We have help on the way.

Reverend Ples is sending manpower which will do as Mr. Black says and a "Mr. Big Shine and his men, will transport necessary light poles. Some of Reverend Ples' men are accomplished electricians and plumbers. Ya'll are to give an estimate on how, what, when you need, and where to store all the items, and they'll unload. Mr. Black, if you will go by Walker Lumber and get them to cut what you'll need they will begin cutting. Place out of Nashville will ship by way of the Southern Railroad, concrete, bricks, and necessary tools."

Amazement was shown on the faces of those present. Then laughter! Wow they exclaimed! Heidi with her lack of knowledge of English, just smiled. Usually in a crowd she just cast her mind in the sea of memories of her love---Billy Ray. She knew a beautiful house would be built and Billy Ray would be proud, but for now her pride was in the magnificent Sissy, the true "Scarlett O'Hara." Sissy had saved the day she assumed.

Sissy continued, "A place in Evansville, Indiana, named Whirlpool are going to send necessary units to air-condition the place. Once we receive deliverance, they'll dispatch men to install. Again Cheers! "Now looking over these blueprints, I agree on what you have rendered. However, this is not my place. Please explain to Heidi about the meanings of each sketch. We'll need to borrow these blueprints later when we go to market to purchase furniture." She said.

Mr. Tuthill asked the question all wanted to know. "Are they properly funded for all of this? What you've explained in the planning and on this blueprint, will be very costly. Normally we can quote by square footage, but you've gone in a direction we are not accustom to."

Mr. Tuthill, in being defensive for Heidi and Billy Ray, I'll just tell you this: A. Before Billy Ray departed and after their marriage, he went to the bank and using his savings and stocks as collateral, was told he would be able to obtain a very   substantial home building loan. He already owned the land. B. In the event of his death while in combat or traveling to -and -from, the insurance on the loan would be valid. C. Payments will be paid weekly by the bank. D. Any, and all workers will be paid."

Landscaping and foundation pouring would commence at once. Next, upon receiving the brick, cement, etc. construction would begin. Oak lumber, using the estimated amount needed from the blueprints, would begin "slabbing" at once. All excess lumber planks were to be stored for future use by Billy Ray.

Orders were submitted the next morning by Mr. Tuthill and Mr. Black. Their reputations were better than a purchase order. The title of the house was "The Coleman Landing". Imagination from all who attended the meeting as well as from Reverend and Daisy Pleasant, plus the love they all had for Billy Ray, just told them this house would be the most beautiful home in Colbert county.

CHAPTER
THIRTY-SIX

Billy Ray, sitting on a coil of rope on the dock waiting on whomever was picking him up and taken to his airplane, realized he was extremely hungry and thirsty. To make matters worse, the environment was smelling good from whatever was being prepared somewhere.
Like a hound dog from back in Alabama, he stood and turned his body, especially the nose, in a manner to identify where the aroma was coming from. At last he decided it was coming from an area near an alley.
At that moment, a young couple from that area, came toward him smiling. "Hallo, my name is Yosef Ulrich and this is my wife Martina. We've been dispatched to collect you. Could we invite you to join us for a meal?"

They shook hands, smiling at each other, and his southern genteel manners took over and his strong urge for food amplified his lack of defense and he responded, "Yes I would love to join you for a meal. You are very kind to invite me."

Are agents for the foreign underground O.S.S. Recruited by General Donovan while they were in college, were trained by experienced agents. From the University of London, their-major had been foreign languages. Martina's disciplines with "agency" were medical and explosives. His were hand-to-hand combat, management, and espionage. They were a great team, one that like Billy Ray, would be used in important projects and political involvement.
The report from Mr. St. Jean to General Donovan on Billy Ray, indicated politically he would grade highly. But on "street¬wise" he needed to be taught more. Knowing Billy Ray's mission, alarmed Mr. St. Jean to the point he felt that he'd never make it past Lisbon.

Yosef and Martina were contacted to get him out of Lisbon and stay with him until he left for England. They too, would receive the Russian training. A twin engine de Havilland was confiscated in France and flown to Lisbon. Extra space would be needed and they would leave it with the Russians once their training was completed. They would return on a merchant ship. Billy Ray would return on U. S. Army aircraft out of Helsinki. It was felt by General Donovan to render him unconscious while in Lisbon, because he would react strongly and cause the mission to be in danger. In addition, his demeaner could cast him in harm's way and he could be slain. Yosef also didn't want him to take the controls of the twin-engine because he'd only been checked out with a single-engine. Yosef was checked-out.

BILBOA, SPAIN

They landed in a rain storm which was to their advantage. They taxied into a very old hanger and unloaded the knocked-out American into an ancient truck. Placing him, still bound with the ropes and tape, in the back of it. Meantime, while the plane was being "topped-out", and the waiting for the storm to pass, all were transported a short distance to a Rabbi's home. There a group of bearded Spanish men untied him, undressed and cleaned him and then redressed the sleeping man. Martina entered the room and gave another injection that woke him up. Immediately, he sprung from the bed and headed for Yosef.

The men grasped him while an exclamation was given. "Billy Ray, Martina and I work for General Donovan also. We were ordered from him, via Mr. St. Jean, not to let you leave alone and more important in a small single engine plane. The weather forecast determined rainstorms were imminent. tie "borrowed" the twin-engine to make this trip. Martina and I will be going with you to our destination. I'll fly but on our way, I'll teach you how to pilot a twin-engine. Arrangements there have been made for the changes made. Billy Ray calmed down.
Now that you understand this, may I begin teaching you some other lessons?"

"Yes" answered the bewildered Billy Ray.
"Please don't be offended, but stop being so nice. Forget your courtly manners, stop smiling so much. Never, Never, take someone at

face value as you did when you met my wife and me. Always carry a weapon for protection if nothing else. You have nothing except your fist and as you can see these men surrounding you would tear you apart if I wasn't here. Stare into the eyes of anyone you meet from now on. No initial smiles, especially to the Russian marines and sailors. They would regard this as a sign of weakness. You are going to be the first American those you will be fighting with or learning from and they will try you. Don't accept help from anyone but Martina and me."

A lugar, nine- millimeter pistol, with holster was given to him along with a full box of ammunition. One old man wearing a black pill box hat, handed him a six -inch throwing knife and some type of pocket knife. Billy Ray nodded thanks, but no smile and looked him straight in the eyes.

Someone banged on the door and when the Rabbi opened it, a message was passed. He spoke to Yosef in Yiddish, and beckoned for Billy Ray to follow. As the men exited, the old man touched Billy Ray on the arm and said "Shalom." Billy Ray didn't look back nor utter a sound. Outside, Yosef mentioned they would be meeting Martina at the plane and they would be flying out soon for Bordeaux, France.

Once on board, he found his duffle bag that disappeared when he initially was rendered out of it.

CHAPTER

THIRTY-SEVEN

Arriving in Helsinki, he was taken back in that he wouldn't be boarding a U. S. Army DC-10, but rather a C-47 Douglas. Piloting was a civilian, or so it seemed, who had a personality. "Welcome aboard Lieutenant, my name is Jose Canto, from Los Angles, where are you from?"

"Uh-Uh, Memphis" "Going home?"

"Don't think so"

"Well take it easy on this trip. In the bulkhead behind my seat is a cot. In addition, there is food in the 'fridge behind the bulkhead wall. Hanging on the rack is extra blankets and a big leather jacket. Could get cold if we need to climb higher. Feel free to use."

"Thanks, will do"

"By the way, here are orders for you. Someone from M16 brought them by."

"Thanks again." "Don't mention it"

Powerful motors were gunned and rev', Billy Ray, finding food and drink, settled down and begin enjoying himself, until Jose told him to "please buckle up, we are takin' off." After they were airborne and not climbing anymore, Billy Ray continued his meal. Sooo!! glad to eat American food again. For the last five weeks, beets, kraut, potatoes and hard bread had been his daily food. Occasionally he got eggs, but the Russians simply didn't know how to properly cook eggs. A bottled Coca-Cola, cooled and fresh, brought his taste buds to a new level. He drank two, back to back.

He opened an envelope from M-16 and began to read:
1. A courier would pick him up upon landing.
2. He would be taken to a place called Clapton South deep-level shelter, in South London, England. (Obviously, this was a tunnel. O.K. by him hope they had made a place for him to sleep and shower)
3. Food and drink would be available.
4. Tomorrow morning, a representative from M16, (England's secret intelligence service) would collect him, and brought to headquarters for indoctrination.
5. Fresh clothing available.

After eating his meal, he went to the cot, covered up and went sound asleep. Hours later they made a petrol stop and with permission, dismounted from the plane and made a bathroom stop. They were in some place that could be a French speaking country. He asked no one nor even cared. Mountains were to the south of him and the buildings were new. Tarmac seemed to be freshly paved. Petrol trucks were decaled with Shell logo. Automobiles were combination of French and German. Peugeot, Citroen and Volkswagen, and parked in the lot near the hanger.

Now on the last leg of the trip, he noticed more people now had joined him for trip to England. The fuselage was now showing at least twenty more people. He just nodded and smiled at them. No conversation.

He sat next to a window, but first he retrieved the large leather coat with the furry lamb's wool- insert, and put it on.
A few hours later, they landed at Heathrow airport in London. He exited at the moment he heard a noise hooking to the fuselage. An English air-force officer opened the door from the outside. Waiting at the bottom of the steps of the aluminum ladder that was set up for use by the planes occupants, was a young Naval officer who asked if he was Billy Ray Coleman.

Answering in the affirmative, the man, obviously an American, exclaimed that he also worked for General Donovan, and had heard about him from the General. Billy Ray just nodded. The Navy officer climbed onboard and took his seat. The pilot and the co-pilot exited also and walked with Billy Ray to transportation available. The pilots got in an old Austin, while he, after being acknowledged by an English junior officer, was hustled off to a Rolls. He was then taken to the tunnel and escorted to the opening by a woman security guard. She locked him in and guarded, from her car, all night duties.

Billy Ray descended the one hundred, eighty steps to the bottom and his room for the evening, was easy to find. He'd heard the front door being locked as he began his first steps. Feeling safe, yes. Liking it, no. He still had his leather coat on and wasn't going to return it. He'd suffered cold weather enough. If he could find proper gloves, he'd steal them too. Such are the spoils of war.

CHAPTER
THIRTY-EIGHT

In the files and orders that Billy Ray had been given from General Donovan and that had been folded so small and waterproofed, were hidden inside the rubber heels of his boots. Thank God for "onion skin paper" he thought as he unfolded them.

Order number one — meet Sr. Lt. Viktor Leonov in Turku, Finland. Runs operation like you had in Bama. Only his is tough. Observe, but don't ask questions. He'll explain. Hd-2- Hd. Special. Live and fight if necessary with them. Do as he leads. People don't get killed with him. Navy/Coast Guard/Marine. Scuba diver. Learn this. One mean s.o.b.
Order number two—Learn explosives and artillery
Order three—Be with him for at least a month
Order four—Learn basic training methods we can use. Order five—pray.
WD/usa

They were picked up by a group of heavily armed sailors, who started placing their hands wrongfully on Martina. Without waiting on Yosef, Billy Ray knocked two of them out. The others pinned him on the deck of the truck until they arrived at the Naval base. Once there, the ranking officer, whom was not knocked out jumped from the back and ran as fast as he could to an intimidating commanding officer. They discussed the situation for a moment and then asked the two men that were knocked out to join him. As they faced him at attention, the officer took from his overcoat pocket a twelve- inch whip and began thrashing the two men who didn't resist. They just took their discipline. They were knocked to the ground and just laid there bleeding. Finally, he stopped and sent his aide to fetch the traveling party.

The three walked casually to this man with the black beard, black hair, thick black eyebrows and a curl on his lips. Billy Ray had determined he would not be treated as the two previous sailors. Through an interpreter speaking a smidgen of German and a large amount of English, began asking questions.

"Are you Coleman"

"Yes"

"Did you do to those men what you've been accused of?"

"Yes"

"Do you have anything to say before sentence is given"

"What sentence. I just defended my comrades as any sailor would."
In speaking this he stared into the darkest eyes he'd ever seen.

The interpreter narrated,

Billy Ray asked "Is this gentleman Lt. Viktor Leonov?" Leonov answered

"Yah"

Billy Ray continued, "My country, the United States of America, have sent me to learn as much as I can from what is considered the greatest fighting man in the world. And to show you my personal gratitude, here are the keys to the de Havilland aircraft I flew here. It now belongs to you as you wish."
He handed him the keys. No smiles from either man.
Leonov spoke to the interpreter again and at length.

"The Lieutenant appreciates your generosity, but his men have asked for satisfaction for the way you caused them trouble."

"How do they want satisfaction?"

"Knives- to death"

He knew he couldn't give in but as he turned to seek counsel from Yosef, he found they were gone. The dagger that he found under his door was in a scabbard he'd made and wrapped and tied on the back of his neck. In his pocket was the old knife the ancient Jew had given him earlier. He knew he must depend on it. At once, he was pushed into a sandy fighting area and the two men started trotting at him. In native American form, he crouched, reached behind his neck, withdrew the dagger and again using velocity as his ally, threw it into the body of the approaching enemy. The assailant screamed and fell back. The other opponent turned to face his friend, giving Billy Ray time to withdraw his pocketknife and open the blade. The Russian turned back toward Billy Ray and pulled his own dagger to finish the American. Charging upright, gave Billy Ray an opportunity to drop down, kick up into the face of his opponent and knock him backwards. Billy Ray jumped on top of him and inserted the blade in his neck. This man died also.

Silence was the order of the day it seemed. No one in the Spetsnaz had ever seen one of their comrades taken down in hand-to-hand combat.

Leonov directed through the interpreter for Billy Ray to join him in his cabin. Nothing changed when they entered except he gave instructions where Billy Ray would inhabit and who would be his interpreter. Billy Ray asked through the interpreter what had happened to his companions. Nothing was said except they were alive.

VIKTOR LEONOV

A master at preparing sailors for combat during the second world war. His methods, not only unorthodox, but hazardous gave his students (sailors) opportunities to win in all endeavors. His groups known as Spetsnaz, learned that being in top physical condition was always mandatory. Proficiency using any type of weapon must be accomplished but the skills to be used with them should be second nature. They were always required to follow his mission plans to an exact.

In addition to all of this, they should be prepared at a moment notice to attack. Being an old Russian sailor, he was always over the top using the new sailors. Viktor was a pioneer in the art of amphibious warfare. Made no difference to him, small campaign or a battle of thousands, he demanded to win and not to lose any of his men. They were equally adept in the use of artillery, explosives, guerilla squadron attacking, and used the most trained special operations forces during this time.

Throughout the short -time Billy Ray served with Spetsnaz, Leonov single-handed led his men on dozens of raids on German bases along the Russian and Finnish coastlines, in the freezing Baltic sea at times. Deploying by inflatable raft, torpedo boat, submarines and even parachuted into snow banks, they wiped out a Nazi communication-center, anti¬aircraft guns, ammunition depots and much more. He taught his men and Billy Ray how to monitor enemy ships and Billy Ray taught them about sonar and radar. Through the leadership of Viktor Leonov, along with Norwegian commandos, destroyed a motor transport depot, killing one hundred, putting out of commission twenty -five trucks and ignited an entire fuel dump. Billy Ray was with him and that night learned about high speed attacking. No one was lost that night.

Billy Ray worked with the Russians for five weeks. It took time but they eventually embraced his friendship. Respect had always been there after he made a stand for himself upon his arrival. Leonov called him in and made startling statements.

First, arrangements had been made for him to travel to Helsinki to catch a U. S. Army DC-Ten for England. Second, he'd been awarded the Bravery-Valor ribbon from Russia. It was named appropriately the Spetsnaz star. He was proud of both announcements.

The next day he was taken by truck to Helsinki's airport. The truck driver gave him a letter from Leonov but wasn't allowed to read it to him..

CHAPTER

THIRTY NINE

Billy Ray knew as he touched with his last step while going down the tunnel, claustrophobia was entering his brain. But that wasn't all entering his thinking and emotion abilities. His self- evaluation was doing strange tricks to the point he felt he was going crazy. Therefore, some type of cathartic maneuver was needed. But what? Why is this happening, how was he to stop it.

"Lord show me a way to overcome this strange malady. My thoughts are so mixed-up." He prayed.
He knelt near his cot and with the help of God, began to begin the purgative method. it was now or never. If something wasn't done now, he would sink further and never return.

Killing so much in the past three years, was what seemed to be the main problem. He wasn't reared to be a killer, but to stand up for himself. He was a military man and did as ordered, but serving in the 155' Russian navy and the joy they took in slaughter went against his Christian training and beliefs.
Brother Edwards at the First Baptist Church in Tuscumbia and his Sunday school teacher, Mike Schrader, had taught him how to conduct his life. Clear biblical points were made. But didn't "thou shall not kill" include even in combat. Answer was NO.

As dastardly as it was, you had to protect those you had sworn to defend. You must purge this nightmare NOW. With all of lessons you had learned from Bud and Sissy, your friends and co-workers, and even your enemies, you were taught difference from right and wrong. Your school teachers not only taught you but directed through people like a man he respected, but didn't like, Ernest Hemingway who once said, "The world breaks everyone and afterward some are strong at the broken places." Okay he understood that, be strong. And William Shakespeare, "Doubt thou the stars are on fire, doubt that the sun doth move, Doubt truth to be a liar, but never doubt I love." Yeah, got that too. I Love my fellow man. I Love Heidi. I Love God. He also was reminded a quote from Gandhi that went, while he shushed some doubters, by saying "The best way to find yourself is to lose yourself in the service of others."

This he understood completely. Serve God and his fellow man. In his remembrance of his past life, he ostensibly felt he was going back to it. But prayer must be uttered came a voice and a strange light that was in his room. It's an epiphany he surmised. Must follow through with thought and prayer, "Be strong, love often and much more through service, were the thoughts. He prayed "Lord, forgive me, love me, lead and guide me. Help me find my way. Help those I love, especially Heidi. Let me be of service to you and my fellow man." Amen.

He repeated this again and again. Finally, warmth sent from God, began the potential release from being poignant. Slowly a smile came to his face. Thinking of Doughbelly, Spider, Monkey, Little Red, Pepper, Eddie, Rex, and the infamous Bones. Laughter started it and then the implosion. He found himself rolling on the cot, leaping in the air, running up and down the steps, ranting as if he had lost his mind. In fact, though, he had never felt so sane. Love came out all over his body Strength.

He was placed in a beat-up pickup truck and taken to an airport for a flight to Dublin, Ireland he was told. Placed in his hands was a file that, apparently, he'd never read. He was left alone to study the contents while the aircraft was being readied for flight when they arrived. The file revealed the remainder of his training and what he would he required to do. It was directly sent to him from General Donovan, coded-translated and typed by someone from M16. Billy Ray had refused to elaborate his training in Finland unless General Donovan gave him a direct order. It was in the file. He knew he must discern the orders, because knowingly General Donovan, some of the pertinent information would still be coded. I.E., word tattoo meant these orders are authentic.

Simply the orders read, he was to study under Lt. Colonel Blair "Paddy" Mayne, a hero from North Africa battles. Primarily about speed fighting using vehicles.

Next, he was to leave Ireland in ten days and go to Quebec City, in Canada. Flight service would be at the local U. S. Army airfield. Upon arrival in Canada, he was to go to Canadian air Base for flight to Helena, Montana. There you will be picked up by a representative of Lieutenant Colonel Robert T. Frederick and taken to him at Fort Harrison. You must present to him, a plan of instruction on what you've learned in Finland and Ireland. This mode of training will be used for the First Special Services force, that consisted of troops from Canada and the United States. They were to go on a very special commando mission. It was suggested that he learn mountain-climbing technics, snow skiing, and repelling. Traveling with the First Special Forces to Europe for the project was a volunteer action from him. Upon completion of this assignment he would be granted a month's pass and could go back home if he desired. Either the Coast Guard or O.S.S., would contact him for future orders.

BIOGRAPHY OF LT. COLONEL BLAIR MAYNE
AKA: "Paddy" Ireland's wolf of the desert was born in Newtownards, Ireland. Never married nor children. Present rank: Lieutenant Colonel. When the nineteen, thirty-eight, Munich crisis occurred, Subject was already a student at the Queen's University Officer Training Corps. Commissioned into the 5th Light Anti-Artillery Territorial Regiment much to the chagrin of his superiors. They had ruled him "unruly and generally unreliable." When war was declared, Mayne was left behind when his unit was sent to Egypt. The snub made an impression on the fearless and lethal but hard-drinking and undisciplined soldier. The commandos accepted him and when Hitler's armies overran continental Europe, Mayne began his brutal physical training , becoming a weapons expert, learned map-reading, Olympic type swimming, rock climbing, practicing unarmed combat using explosives and importantly, how to organize transportation in all situations, He was deadly now.
In his first assignment in Syria, one hundred and twenty British soldiers were killed. Mayne became angry at his commanding officer for not including him on the roster of a raid to abduct Rommel, which was never carried out, due to the efficiency of Lt. Colonel Geoffrey Keyes. Irked at Mayne, the "Colonel" approached Mayne one evening in the mess hall, and proceeded to "chew him out." The resentful Irishman rose from his chair and knocked Keyes senseless with a roundhouse right to the jaw. His next commanding officer would be much wiser in using the Irish's deadly

talents.

Colonel David Stirling placed Paddy in a battle almost at once and allowed him to proceed at will. From his perspective, Paddy began using more speed by utilizing the American made "Jeep". This way they could attack Luftwaffe units. Using the Jeeps, the commandos, aka SAS, swiftly outfitted Paddy's group. They welded two Vickers machine guns facing forward on the vehicles and a swiveling fifty -caliber Browning in the rear, that transformed the machines into devastating, high-speed gun platforms. Mid -year of nineteen forty-two the unit was wholly motorized and ready to strike with Paddy Mayne as it's leader.

On July fourth, an SAS convoy set out to raid the airfields scattered in the Bagush/Fuka region, one hundred miles behind enemy lines. Reaching Bagush on the night of July seventh, Mayne and three men blew up twenty-two aircraft with plastic explosives. His was far fewer than they had sabotaged, and Mayne growled, "Man we did forty aircraft. Some of the primers must have been damp." He just wasn't someone to leave the job undone, Mayne and Stirling charged their vehicles onto the airfield and opened- up with their Vickers guns, firing one thousand, two hundred rounds per minute apiece.

Stunned by this new assault after they assumed the saboteurs had departed, the Nazi ran for cover as the British Raiders shot to pieces twelve more of the Luftwaffe's precious warplanes.

During this time, he received a promotion to Captain and awarded the Distinguished Service Order.

Many more successful raids were made. They needed to be because Rommel's Tobruk offensive on one occasion, resulted in capturing Thirty-three Thousand prisoners, including five generals and a tremendous cache of tanks, artillery, food and Medicine. Mayne saved the day and one Billy Ray needed to learn from.

He studied on and on and was relieved when in two hours they landed in Dublin. Billy Ray exited the air-liner wearing the leather, wool- lined bomber jacket.

There waiting for him was Colonel Mayne, drunk as he could be.

CHAPTER
FORTY

He couldn't believe his eyes. A colonel in mid-day drunk, weaving and swirling. Just as he began descending, the British Military Police arrived and arrested Mayne. For future commitments and meetings, he pretended he didn't see what was going on. The police quickly got the Colonel out of the public's eyes and left Billy Ray standing alone. The Colonel's driver approached Billy Ray and said he'd take care of him and would dispatch him to officer's quarters. He needed to change into American uniform once he arrived. The driver would go in with him as he sought a Coast Guard Uniform. If one was not available he'd need to secure one for the young hero. As it turned out he did in fact have one but he needed it pressed.

The driver took care of it and returned in thirty minutes with it pressed and brass polished. His ribbons were okay.
A Major sought him out later and escorted him to officer's mess hall for dinner. People who worked for General Donovan were present and would undergo the same training. Only problem was the host would he be in good enough shape to educate them. After the meal, he was sent back to the barracks and was told that he'd he picked up at seven o'clock and to be ready and wear utilities. Leave duffle bag and contents in the same place as where he spent the night. A new brief-case would be given to him so that he could store paper-work and items.

Sleep came easy this night, but at five o'clock a.m., two men woke him up and directed him to come with them for transportation to meet with Lt. Colonel Blair Mayne for breakfast. This he did but wasn't smiling. How dare him to get drunk and stand him up one day, miss dinner meeting and then have someone awake him so early in the morning. It was time for a "showdown"

He marched into the mess hall at full military prance. Stopping just a few feet from Paddy Mayne, came to attention, popped a salute and reported "Sir, Lieutenant Billy Ray Coleman, reporting as ordered, sir." He stared into the Colonel's blue eyes and held them. The Colonel returned the salute and motioned for him to sit. This he did. But he didn't speak.

The Colonel began the conversation.

"Young man, why are you here?"

"Sir it's this way, I have the strength to change. My country desires to change not only culturally but militarily. So, they have delegated me to learn as much as possible, especially among top military people such as yourself. Your strong reputation in North Africa battles have reached our shores and your methods of spirited warfare is what we are looking for. I have recently served in another country with a tremendous leader and if I'm not incorrect you too are such a leader. I wish to learn from you so that I can place both of your lessons together for future instruction. However, for the short time I'll be here, it is imperative that you remain sober and teach me forthright. Recently I've been on the edge of emotion, nearly mentally - bankrupt. Don't intend to let anything else happen mto me, because I have many men to train, using your methodsmand the other instructor I had. We need to win this war and stop it. Don't you agree?"

"Aye lad aye."

"And you will be with and for me for next ten days?"

"Aye lad Aye."

"Is it possible to start today?"

Again, "Aye lad Aye."

They walked out to the Jeep upon completion of breakfast. Mayne then began his dissertation on fast attacks. Perhaps Paddy thought for a moment that he was working on his Phd. Regardless, things must begin at once. He'd compromise if he only realized what he must learn.

At the hanger, Paddy started teaching him what he and Stirling together. In looking the young man over, he figured this individual was no fool and he swore to himself to refrain from drinking and instruct him correctly.

More and more, daily grind, no trivial, no transgressions ten days and then they were through. Time to stop and go to America. Oh! How he rejoiced.

CHAPTER

FORTY-ONE

Apparently General Donovan using his power with the President, requested cooperation from the Army Air Force and received it with other needs for Lieutenant Billy Ray Coleman to spare. He was flown directly from Northern France to Quebec City in Canada, with a Doctor and full medical team. They attended to his needs and within a short distance across the Atlantic Ocean, he was up and observing the convoy of fighter planes escorting them.

A male nurse asked, "Sir, are you some kind of a hero? We don't give this attention to anyone except medal of honor winners."
"Don't think I'm getting the medal. Know I don't deserve it anyhow. Just fighting with a foreign power."
When they landed in Quebec, a detail of "Mounties" unloaded him from the de Havilland onto a small four-seater Cessna, for flight to Fort Harrison in Helena, Montana.

Once they arrived there, he was picked up in the "General's limousine" and taken directly to "General's Headquarters " Now the entrance was typical but going through the inner door was an anomaly unlike anything that had ever occurred to him before. It was the most faux office set up of all time. The guide and he walked on through the "General's" office desk area, where a retired Colonel sat, doing nothing, smiling at all who entered as they made their way on through and exited to a real office area, that would be a combination meeting room and two large desks. One for Lieutenant Billy Ray Coleman, U.S. Coast Guard (O.S.S.), Training Officer-in-charge and one for Lieutenant Colonel

Robert T. Fredrick, U.S. Army, the true officer-in-charge of Fort Harrison and commander of the First Special Services Force. These were the only commanders that conversed about present and future activities. The "General" was for show only. He met with community leaders, took care of any local activities, and attended parades. The premise told to the media from him was one that addressed paratroop and mountain-climbing was one of aiding the Canadian military. No conversation between the two leaders and the "General" ever existed.

Before Billy Ray explained his training methods to anyone, he opened the wall safe that contained an enigma, and coded message to General Donovan. In it he explained who he'd been with, what they did, where they had performed, how they had been successful. Farther, gave present address and what he was doing. Knowing the General was aware of his physical condition, explained he was doing fine and began work.

To which someone sent him information about to whom and with whom he would interact. Biography of individuals and men of his group contained:

1. Lord Louis Mountbatten and Lt. Colonel Robert T. Frederick, Commanders

2. Dossier on Frederick, reflected grad of West Point, born in San Francisco, staff officer of War Department, Inventor of the V-42 combat knife, expert in parachuting and upon landing, immediate fast attack. Also, instrumental in inventing the M1941 Johnson machine gun. Was the recruiter for this unit which consisted of three small regiments, a service battalion. (approximately 1800 men) mostly volunteer military men that had been previously employed as forest rangers, hunters, game wardens, lumberjacks, and high-profile skiers. Boxers, athletes, and sharpshooters were welcomed also. Frederick wanted his men to be aware of the fighting prowess of these troops.

3. Mission would include many locations and required strength and comradeship. Reason as to why Canadians: A could and should join was obvious.

4. Mountbatten had selected Frederick and taught how he wanted. A source to be reckoned with. Even though he was royalty, he was trained highly in the Royal Navy and had served as Captain of ships and massive training of British sailors. He was the Father of the commando training.

5. Lt. Coleman will publish for the training manuals of this group,

in concert with Colonel Frederick, how to be properly trained using tactics learned in European theaters.

6. Writer will join you before training has eclipsed.
Billy Ray, getting hungry, went back out the front door and asked where the mess hall was located and how he could find transportation to it. The guard he asked, told him to wait and went inside for only a few seconds. Upon returning, he informed Billy Ray to wait there and an auto would soon pick him up. This was done and even though he was nursing a wound, he wore his class "A's" with only rank showing. After he sat down, a young enlisted man wearing chef whites, asked him how he wanted his steak cooked. Further if the Lieutenant wanted baked potato or country French fries. He answered and sat in awe at the prospect of eating American meat again.

While waiting, a Corporal came over and inquired where he wanted his Dictaphone placed, what his clothing/boot size were, and if he needed personal hygiene items from the PX.
Billy Ray answered and asked some questions of his own. Like barbershop, personal transportation, and arms room. The corporal told him he was the Lieutenant's concierge and would take care of his details. Going back to the office, the Corporal would stop by the barbershop and the Doctor's office for information as to necessities. He had been issued his own car now and he would be taken care of properly.

The concierge would see to it. After consuming the wonderful meal, he left to do a lot of errands. Find and see the doctor. Bandages need to be changed. Locate his living quarters and have duffle bag delivered there. He kept his rucksack with him wherever he went. Get a needed haircut. The Corporal told him his utilities/fatigues, would be delivered to his quarters along with new boots. Buy items at PX. Meet the chaplain. Pick up weapons. Corporal said the Lieutenant's name was on approved list. Get new identification card. Return to office to meet his commanding officer.

Duties were many but getting started with the manual was top priority. He returned to his office and found two interesting instruments, one mechanical and the other deadly.

Perched next to his chair was a new Dictaphone. Something he'd never operated, but sure the Corporal would show him. But first he needed to learn his name and if in fact he was doing. Knowing the General was aware of Mission would include many locations and required strength and comradeship. Reason as to why Canadians: Army could and should join was obvious.

4. Mountbatten had selected Frederick and taught how he wanted. A source to be reckoned with. Even though he was royalty, he was trained highly in the Royal Navy and cleared to associate with now. Nice guy, but still noteworthy in this field of espionage.

In the middle of his wooden desk was a V-42 combat knife stuck as if it had been thrown. This weapon was the trademark of the 1" Special Service Force, and apparently, Lt. Colonel Frederick would agree with him to use it extensively, therefore he would incorporate it when ascertaining certain hand-to-hand maneuvers. He pulled it from its position and looked it over. Short-bladed stiletto with a thumb groove on the top of the blade to promote proper hand placement when attacking an opponent. It was introduced by Colonel Frederick, who he'd been the inventor of it.

Someone was trying to give him messages. The Corporal's name was Ian Ingalls of the Canada Joint Task Force Two, part of the 1" Special Service Force, service battalion. Funny, Billy Ray thought he'd heard that name before. Big blond guy with strange accent. But from Canada, he'd heard many strange accents. Cleared for top secret, from information package he'd found in the vault. He'd verify later.

While his back was turned, looking in the vault, he sensed someone walking toward his rear. Instinctively, finding a pistol on a shelf In the vault, he spun around and went to the floor, taking an aim at a startled Lt. Colonel, who shouted "Don't shot. Don't shoot Billy Ray." Luckily the shoot safety was on because Billy Ray was squeezing the trigger. He continued squeezing until the voice became real to him. "Sorry Lieutenant didn't mean to sneak up on you."

"My, apologizes, sir; should've been aware that only you would be entering these chambers."

"Man, you are scary, sure you don't want to go back to Europe with us?"

"Sir I'm a military man, I go where I'm sent. However, I'm also a political servant also. Go where I'm sent there too. Soo! I stay mixed-up most of the time. (Laughter), Hope you can teach me how to operate this Dictaphone, it isn't military or political." (laughter again)

"I'll try."

CHAPTER

FORTY-TWO

In his time alone at Fort Harrison, during the time he was editing his manual for commandos, he went back in his memories and recalled the day of his fist battle at sea in the gulf of Mexico. He was serving for the first time as captain of a cutter......THE HAIDA.....the fateful day even stronger as when he and the Alabama boys stopped the Nazi commandos at the Battle of Wilson Dam.

Oh! How he missed the men he'd served with in land and sea combat. And to think he'd never lost a man.

Tears flowed tremendously in the though of war. Hurt of not seeing his friends. Now he was training hard with American and Canadian men to fight and to survive. Oh! How bad he wanted them to survive.

The tears subsided and laughter arose when his memory came back about his learning how to fly an airplane. How inept he was . But the war on the Gulf would never leave him. On a starry night as he was in such a mood, examination of things that had been worrying him the most like the loss of Gloria, fighting the Nazi in Alabama, gulf war slaughter, killing two Russians in hand to hand combat, and serving with Mayne was beginning to take its toll. At times he was in traumatic syndrome and he wanted to shut it off and began thinking good thoughts of Heidi and his experiences with Yosef and Martina .

"Excellent " said Martina. "We are having Shashuka and grape juice. Since Shabbat, our cupboards are lean., but I think you will enjoy this meal." He just nodded his approval, not knowing what Shashuka or Shabbat was. As they entered their apartment, Yosef handed Billy Ray, a "beannie" or Yamaka are directed him to wear it. Made no difference to him, just being there to eat was all he had on his mind.

They sat at a small table after prayers were said in Yiddish, they began to eat. The meal was warm and consisted of poached eggs on a tomato paste bed. The drink was cooled but no ice. He ate with gusto alike Doughbelly once did. Just the consuming of this delicious food reminded him of his friends from the past.

Contentment overcame him and he began to get sleepy. "Could you direct me to an area where I could was my face, getting sleepy?" Nothing though, just silence. Perhaps didn't understand the question he thought. "Yosef, got to go to bathroom, where are the facilities?" Again silence. He stood for only a second and then passed out.

He was out a long time it seemed and awoke bounded on his wrists and ankles with rope. A vile tasting wide tape over was his mouth. His eyes weren't covered and the feel plus ability to look around told him that he was on the floor of an airplane flying at a great speed. He realized that Yosef was piloting and Martin was assisting him with maps. Each wore leather helmets that contained microphones. He also realized he'd we his trousers and due to the height, he was very cold and his jaw trying to chatter. He thrashed about and tried scream out but to no avail, He was ignored for a while. Between the jerks of his thrashing about, he realized Yosef was talking to someone somewhere else. Aha! He thought, we are in a twin engine plane and not a single-engine plane he'd been taught to fly. Descending rapidly and picking up rain was happening. He began moaning loudly and shaking so hard that he was rocking the plane. Martina turned to observe and made a fateful decision. Opening her purse, she pulled out a "loaded" syringe and inserted the contents into Billy Ray's arm. He temporary went back to an unconscious state.

CHAPTER

FORTY-THREE

Funny thing about men from this era, in that telling someone good bye wasn't a requirement in manners. Instead of shaking hands or "hugs," they just nodded at each other. If a woman like you a lot you could receive a hug or sometimes a kiss.

Billy Ray, upon leaving, told Paddy Mayne farewell with a hand shake. This was his way and he always complied with the gentleman's code. Now that his attitude was as it should be. He was ready now to do the plan of training from what he'd been taught and experienced.
He had been assigned to a new brigade that was being formed at Fort Harrison, Montana. It was made up of American "hunk" soldiers and "woodsman" Canadians. They had been trained in basic training and some in advance infantry training.

PLAN OF TRAINING
    1. BE IN TOP PHYSICAL SHAPE:
        A. RUN DAILY AT LEAST THREE MILES PLUS SPRINTS. CARRY RIFLE OVER SHOULDERS UPWARD FOR A MILE.
        B. FIFTY PUSH-UPS PER DAY.
        C. FIFTY SIT-UPS PER DAY.
        D. OBSTACLE COURSE ON ODD-DAY
        E. THROW HEAVY IRON BARS OR BALL PER DAY
        F. SWIM IN COLD WATER IN THE EVENING ON EVEN DAYS.
        G. JUMP OVER FENCE (SIX FEET) WHILE DOING

OBSTACLE COURSE AND BE PREPARED TO THROW EITHER DAGGER OR AXE AT TARGET. TARGETS MUST BE HIT.

2. PRACTICE FIRING WEAPONS DAILY:
    A. THOMPSON MACHINE GUN
    B. "GREASE' MACHINE GUN
    C. .45 PISTOL
    D. M-1 GARAND RIFLE
    E. ALL ROCKET-FIRED WEAPONS
    F. GRENADE FIRING
    G. .50 CALIBER FIRING FROM BACK OF JEEP

3. MANUVERS
    A. ROPE CLIMBING
    B. REPELLING
    C. MOUNTAIN CLIMBING
    D. FIRING .30 CALIBER AND M-1 FROM FOXHOLE, RUNNING, REPELLING AND SWIMMING.
    E. ABILITY TO EAT IN COMBAT -- (c & k RATIONS)
    F. DRIVING JEEPS, TWO-HALF TON TRUCKS, WEAPONS CARRIERS AND TANKS IS A MUST. JEEPS AT TIMES MUST BE DRIVEN WHILE SOMEONE IS FIRING .50 CALIBER STATIONARY MACHINE GUN.
    G. PARATROOP TRAINING

4. FIRST AID
A. NORMAL FIRST AID—USING DRESSINGS.
B. DRESSING WITH SULFA DRUGS
C. PROPER USE OF INJECTED DRUGS, ESPECIALLY MORPHINE.
D. STOPPING BLEEDING
E. STERLIZING INSTRUMENTS
F. PURFIYING WATER
G. BE AWARE OF DEHYDRIATION

You will be taught patterns for survival, psychology of survival, control of natural reactions, Preparing yourself here and now The technics I learned while serving with the Russian Navy and with British Empire desert attacks will be implemented and you will be afforded how to win in combat plus how to survive.

5. SURVIVAL ACTIONS—IN GENERAL
    A. SIZE UP SITUATION
    B. KNOW AND SIZE UP YOUR ENVIRONMENT
    C. RELY ON PHYSICAL CONDITION
    D. KNOW AND SIZE UP WEAPONS AND EQUIPMENT
    E. USE All YOUR SENSES-LEARN HASTE SOMETIMES MAKES WASTE
    F. DON'T FEAR AND PANIC
    G.IF YOU NEED TO, IMPROVISE
    H. KNOW WHAT, WHEN, WHERE, AND HOW
    I. PLACE HIGH VALUE ON LIVING
    J. LEARN BASIC SKILLS BUT LEARN HOW TO LIVE BY YOUR WITS.

6 HAND-TO-HAND-COMBAT
    A. JU JIT SU TECHNICS
    B. KARATE HAND MOVES
    C. CHICAGO STYLE DEFENSE MOVES
    D. HOUSE FIGHTING
    E. KNIFE FIGHTING
    F. STREET FIGHTING AGAINST MORE THAN ONE PERSON
    G. PUNCH TO KNOCKOUT
    H. BOXING

7. SNOW SKIING
    A. GENERAL MOVES
    B. FORREST SKIING
    C. MOUNTAIN SKIING
    D. CROSS COUNTRY SKIING
    E. FIRING WEAPONS WHILE SKIING
    F. CHANGE OVER FROM RUNNING/WALKING TO IMMEDIATE SKIING
8. REST AND RELAXATION
    A. LEARN TO EXIST ON FOUR HOURS SLEEP DAILY
    B. DIGEST FOOD-DON'T "WOLF" IT DOWN

C. FREQUENT URINITATION
D. DAILY BOWEL MOVEMENTS
E. WASH AS MUCH AS POSSIBLE
F. BRUSH TEETH DAILY

You are to win and survive. While serving in Finland lately, my mentor took hundreds of men into combat and annihilated the enemy and seldom lost any of his troops. At another post, I learned how to attack at top speed. My mentor there had invented an entire new form of speed war. You will "TRAIN AND FIGHT TOGETHER."

Key word that'll guide you through all of this is "STEALTH." You are now commandos and will be sent on missions that will require all you learn here and more. GOOD LUCK

CHAPTER

FORTY-FOUR

For over an hour Colonel Frederick and Lieutenant Coleman shared each other biographies. The connection from where Coleman had recently shared to him and the present training tables, fascinated the Colonel even more. Since the security clearance had been lifted by General Donovan and Lord Mountbatten, the two local men found a comradeship that normally would have been clouded. It was get down to work now and they couldn't wait to get training started and end with a high-class assignment.

Frederick and Coleman agreed a joint meeting including staff officers and top NCO'S would be appropriate and to do it at the "General's Headquarters"; would acquaint the staff leaders with Coleman. Knowing it would be at least another week to complete from his outline to printers, he would be another "ghost." Plus, he wanted to be available to answer any questions from the directives he'd include in the training manual.

And so, it was decided to meet tomorrow night, after dinner meal. In the meantime, he'd start translating the outline into the actual recording. Using two Dictaphones, one thin vinyl tapes and the other, the latest, that used magnetic recorders. It was deemed better security to use these as the medium, rather than the old, wax cylinders previously invented.

While dictating the next day, out of the corner of his eye, he noticed Corporal Ingalls standing in the foyer looking in his direction.

Easing up from his desk, he walked into the large-vault and pulled from the two-o-one files hidden in the back section, behind a very thick door, the sought file of Ian Ingalls. Evidence revealed as he thought it would, the proof that the man in question had been at one time a member of the Nazi party. Reading further he put the pieces together that placed him in Muscle Shoals, Alabama at nearly the same time as he put his squadron together to halt the explosion of Wilson Dam and the nitrogen plant. He went back to his desk without the file. There he began dictating again attempting to have Ingalls to place his attention on work in process. After a short time, he stopped dictating and had play-back that still would have same effect, on louder.

Meantime, he slipped out of anyone vision, slipped into the "General's Office" exited through front door that led past the secretary's desk, turned left and stuck his head around the corner wall and saw the Corporal staring through a crack in the wall at Colonel Frederick and his office area. Silently, Billy Ray crept up to him and put the barrel of his weapon behind the Corporal's right ear, and exclaimed, "hold it, raise your hands, and drop to the floor."

This he did. At that moment, the Colonel walked through the front door and appraising the situation, asked "what's going on?"

Billy Ray stated, "Corporal walk on in to my area and sit. Colonel, follow and I'll explain."

"Of course, Billy Ray, I'll follow."

The three men entered with Billy Ray keeping his gun trained on Ingalls. They sat at once.

"Why are you doing this to me?" Ingalls asked. Billy Ray, responded," Colonel, doesn't know much about you and me at a place called,

"Muscle Shoals," on the Tennessee River."

"Oh! I see" replied Ingalls.

"Well, start explaining"

"Could you lower the gun? Makes me nervous" "No, but I'll begin your explanation. It's this way sir,

A couple of years ago, I was trained, along with a group of men from my community, to halt commandos from Germany/Italy, that were sent to explode a group of dams that produced electricity on the Tennessee river. We stopped and captured them in the spring of nineteen, forty- two. In reviewing the roster of those that were to be participants in the battle, one person/name failed to appear. Ian von Ingalls. We searched, but he was never located. I caught this corporal lingering in the hall here observing my functions. I went around to the back of him and captured him. I desire follow-up and wish to know why he is here."

"Don't blame you Lieutenant. Care to explain yourself Corporal?"

"Everything mentioned is correct sir. Remainder of story hasn't been given yet. This is what happened. When my Nazi platoon and I arrived at the railroad shops in Sheffield, Alabama, I realized that there was no way I could be a part of sabotage and kill so many innocent people, I walked and hid away. As my group went down a hill to the river side, I ran backwards to the town of Tuscumbia. Just as I entered the edge of town, I located two houses that were empty. In the small house, I broke in and found refuge. Stayed there for three days, leaving in the darkness to scavenge. Dressed in civilian clothing, ate from garbage cans and bathed at the nearby springs. Wasn't sure as to what I was going to do; but knew for sure I wasn't going to kill Americans. I'd gone to college here and become affectionate to American and democratic ways. Hitler and Nazism, just wasn't what I wanted. Anyway, I left Alabama on tankers, traveled as hobo, hitchhiked on trucks going to Canada and decided to join the Royal Mounties and did so. I was selected to come here due to my ability to speak many languages, including French, English and German."

"O.K., but why were you spying on the Lieutenant as he was dictating?"

"Observing sir. Consider the Lieutenant to be one of the most proficient officers in the United States Military. I wish to pattern myself as him for the Canadian military."

"Very commendable, but why didn't you come forward and seek training the correct way. Now you have established mistrust and I must reassign you. From this day on, you'll go back to the billets and become another member of the First Special Services team. You'll be scrutinized, and you are not to ever mention todays, yesterdays, or future endeavors. But you must run like the Marathoner- Pheidippides, solider like Black Jack Pershing, and lead like Caesar. Do you understand this Corporal?"

"Yes sir."

"Then report to the First Sergeant for assignment. Give me all of your keys."

This he did and left like a hang dog in-route to his cage. Colonel Frederick looking directly toward Billy Ray said, "sorry about all of this, but he is a very good soldier. He'll be placed on the line and later sent to officer candidate school, if, he makes a better showing. I did know about his brief stint in the German Army but didn't realize he'd been cast as enemy/commando to explode our important places that are needed for the war effort. Perhaps this will work out.

Billy Ray dubious about this recent escape, would be on the alert at -all-times. The O.S.S. trained him differently. Ralph Waldo Emerson, said, "Live in the Sunshine, Swim in the sea, Drink the wild air." This applied to civilian lifestyle. But to the military, "win, kill, live and function again." That was what he'd been taught and that was what he believed. Certainly, he believed in God, good life and family. But now we were at war and he intended to return to "Pride's Landing."

THE MANUAL

For the next two days, Lieutenant Billy Ray Coleman dictated the outlines and interpreted for the manual. Finally, he completed his task and called for the printers to relocate and set up in the conference room. This made them unhappy because he watched them all times. In addition to the outlines, he inserted facts, figures and results of the battles he'd been in while participating in Russia, Finland, France and England. He spoke of the factions of the leaders and how they were successful. But as to the two men that taught him so well, he honored them the best he could in the manual's epilogue.

FIRST SERVICE FORCE MANUAL EPILOGUE
MANY MEN WHO TOOK THE TIME AND THE EFFORT TO TEACH THIS WRITER WHO. WHAT. WHEN AND HOW . TO FIGHT THE COMMANDO WAY, THE MOST IMPORTANT Were MARINE LIEUTENANT VIKTOR LEONOV, Russian navy, AND LIEUTENANT COLONEL BLAIR "PADDY"
Mayne of the herald desert fox forces, BRITISH EMPIRE FORCES.

On November 1941, Lieutenant Coleman joined Leonov's detachment that raided the motor transport in the settlement of Titovka. In destroying twenty-five trucks, two fuel storage depots and a storehouse, the detachment also killed over one-hundred enemy soldiers while suffering no loses of their own. In the spring in another raid, the detachment also known as the 181st Special reconnaissance detachment destroyed another enemy depot in the region of Zapandnaya Litsa, killing over seventy German soldiers in the process.

A little over another month another series of successful operations followed. Landing his men from fast torpedo boats, Leonov, with lt. Coleman in tow, secured the landing of the twelve marine Brigade on enemy territory, during which his detachment killed over sixty Germans. The parent organization, the 181" Special Reconnaissance Detachment spent the month destroying enemy anti-aircraft sites, mapping the coastline and capturing prisoners.

After leaving Leonov's detachment, was informed that he led an operation to neutralize a heavy defended-the German artillery emplacement at Cape Krestovy. They had 15CM guns defending the entrance that was very strategically placed. He led a company in a secret landing further along the coast, before undertaking a two-day cross-country. There they captured a battery of 8.8 cm dual purpose guns and used them both to repel a counterattack and to shell the main gun position. This forced the Germans into destroying the coastal guns for the fear of them falling into Soviet hands. For this, Leonov was awarded the hero of the soviet -union.

PADDY MAYNE, JUST AS TOUGH AS LEONOV. EXCELLED IN ATTACKING ON THE DESERT WITH AMERICAN JEEPS, ATTACHED FIFTY CALIBER MACHINE GUNS WELDED TO BACK-SEAT AREA. SPEED WAS THE FACTOR HERE, BUT LATER MAYNE THREW HIMSELF RETRAINING HIS TROOPS FOR NON-DESERT WAREFARE. NOW CALLED THE SAS, NEVER AGAIN REACHED THE HEIGHTS OF GALLANTRY, EFFECTIVENESS AND ADVENTURE IT HADE ACHIEVED IN NORTH AFRICA. COLEMAN JOINED THEM NEAR LE MANS, FRANCE. HE TOOK THEM THROUGH SICILY, ITALY AND INTO GERMANY. THROUGH THOSE THEATRES, MAYNE TRAINED AND LED MANY TROOPS INTO BATTLE. HE CEIVED MANY DECORATIONS, AWARDS, AND PROMOTED.

CHAPTER

FORTY-FIVE

Once the manual was finished in its explanation and printed, Colonel Frederick called a staff officers and top NCO's meeting. Even though he'd been busy in the publication, he didn't fail to get himself in top physical shape. He also kept up with the whereabouts of Corporal Ingalls.

The meeting went well and all of remarks had been exemplary. Physical training was now over and the other high=lights stood out to be addressed. Billy Ray wanted to be a part of remainder but, O.S.S., had other items he was wanted to be a part of.

Orders came down from the Department of Coast Guard, to report to officer — in — charge. He would catch a train for Quebec and then fly to Washington D. C. Spent another two weeks at Fort Harrison reviewing the curriculum and the people and von Ingalls, was retained as member and cadre of this organization. Billy Ray was told that upon completion of the training, this group would be sent to Vermont to under-go skiing activities. From there, to an underdetermined area for combat. Billy Ray departed on time, caught a flight and landed in Washington, D.C. He was happy for Ingalls as well as "Little Shine". Heidi and Jane had written to him about the people he loved or knew about; such as, "Little Shine" who was now in a wonderful school in Nashville that encouraged and taught him about a lot of Social Science. Unfortunately, his Dad, "Big Shine" had been killed in a truck accident. Billy Norman killed in combat while on a patrol in the far east. So far, no reports of the "Alabama Boys" that indicate fatalities or anything detrimental. Commander Moody and Chief Gaskins, still on the job at the academy. Bigbee now was training horses for the U.S. Polo team for next Olympics. Ensign Wright, now an instructor at the Academy and studying proper techniques for operations of larger cutters.

CHAPTER

FORTY-SIX

He arrived in Washington D. C., in complete "Class A" uniform, with national and international medals and badges. He had to be the most decorated coast guardsman in existence. Of course, caught a taxi and loaded his duffle bag, brief case and rucksack. Then was taken into the building that housed the U. S. Coast Guard. Inside were many young personnel that gazed at him and his uniform. In a short time, an ensign approached him to ascertain if there was anything he could do for him. Billy Ray gave him his name and walked to window sash to look out. The ensign walked away and conferred with an older civilian lady

She walked over and introduced herself as Miss Throckmorten and told him to follow her. They walked to a large conference room and he was directed to take a seat, and someone would be with him momentarily.

He waited about an hour, then the door opened and entering was General Donovan. Smiling and looking like a General should, he stuck his hand out for the customary hand-shake. The General saw a "new" Billy Ray Coleman. He asked, "Times have been hard haven't they Billy Ray?"

"That they have General"

"Would you do it over?"

"Probably"

"You've done a great job. I've got your reports and reports from others. Our country is in debt to you. I want you to take a month leave time. Go home and be with your wife. Wait for some orders, but above all relax. You deserve it. I'll call you when I need you. We'll meet at Courtland at a designated time."

"I'll send you home today. Miss Throckmorten has all arrangements made. You should arrive tonight."

"Thank you, sir,"

They shook hands and the General departed.

His flight was on a MAS that landed at several places. He landed at Courtland and checked out an automobile for two days. He drove carefully and good speed.

When he arrived at the turn-off to Pride's Landing, he immediately saw his new home. Awe and bewilderment was what he saw first. Trembling and needing to go to the bathroom caused him to realize that he wanted to hold and kiss her at once. But instead, he did get out of the car in- order to relieve himself. While standing, he again tried to focus on the house. He had a rough time getting back in. However, he drove to the gate that was locked.

He jumped the fence and went to the front porch. He noticed the door was locked, so he jumped off and walked to back of house. What he witnessed was some more beauty. Then went to the back door and looked inside. There he saw his beautiful wife and a black lady he knew as "Daisy", the wife of "Ples". He lightly tapped on the glass pane and the two ladies looked up startled. He placed his face in viewing site and tapped again. This time they recognized him and both screeched. She opened the door, grabbed him around the neck and began kissing him Daisy started jumping up and down. Dogs began to howl, outside alarms went off and birds were chirping loudly.

"My husband, my husband, I'm so glad to see and kiss you."

"My wife, my wife, was all he could say.

That night and the next day, they were inseparable.

Love had never been so grand. Upon the climax of the war, Billy Ray ran for and was elected Probate Judge for Colbert County and later became the leading military man in Alabama.

CHAPTER

FORTY-SEVEN

Voices from his tenure while serving in World War two had lately called to him in dreams around midnight, started to seem too realistic and haunting. However, bugles of the Korean conflict seemed to have a stronger effect on him due to the memories from the stress while patrolling the peninsula and the hailing of firepower dropping near the sea crafts he commanded. That as bad but nothing like the dread of atomic explosions was the ambivalence constantly.

Upon discharge of his tours of duty for the O.S.S. coast guard, he decided to resign from future warfare and returned home to Heidi. Popularity in the political arena dictated he should serve locally and not return to working for the U.S. Postal Service. Push was for him to run for office as county probate judge, which he did, and won by a landslide. But up until the "dreams" appeared, his life had become better. Theory: "all is well that ends well" was not the antithesis, but rather the parallel". Now he could state his position based on legality and not dialog. Trust not misgivings. So much more; not less. Folks in this part of the world knew him for what he was and what he stood for during his many trials and tribulations. He was revered and respected in the communities in his county. But throughout his state as well as most of the nation he was the epitome of the American hero.

Political leaders in this state sought his approval in many situations except for one to be a racist ----they knew he'd never stand for that. Therefore, he wasn't asked. Being a simple common-type man, no drinking, nor braggart, no running around on his wife, just everyday fisherman who went to church and respectful to all, was the way he operated. Before he exited for home each day, the routine was to walk in the perimeter of Spring Park and feed the many ducks located on the bank of the stones placed there by the C.C.C. workers. During this time, he prayed for the events and people he served on this day.

Heidi, his wonderful wife, did not understand the American measured life, but she did understand the power of prayer. Her love and respect she held for him exemplified this devotion. Unfortunately, folks in Colbert County, didn't understand how they made their marriage work since he was a member of the Baptist church and she was a Jew.
It was difficult for her to comprehend why so many people that came back from wars continued in seeking Billy Ray's help in a vast request to look over some laws and to be illegal in their appeal for him to do a law without laws being passed by the legislature. Even last night a stranger knocked on their door and sought an appointment for another man that involved her husband for Saturday morning at a café in Tuscumbia.
Billy Ray with a frown on his brow agreed to have breakfast without conferring with her.

Next morning, he arose early and fed his animals before departing to downtown for his appointment. What Heidi didn't know was he was to meet one of his oldest friends from the military, General Bill Donovan, commandant of O.S.S. (ret)
Meeting place was at Pete's café at 8 o'clock and told her he wouldn't return until about eleven o'clock and would take her on their skiff for a sailing venture complete with a picnic which he'd pick up the food and drink from the Woodymac Drive-in.

He knew once he arrived at Pete's discussion would center around last nights high school football game between arch- rivals Deshler and Sheffield. Radio report was the game had ended in a 13-13 tie. A table of plastic and aluminum decorated in the red-white colors of the Deshler "Tigers". Getting there early rendered for him the habitual plate of three eggs over-light, buttered cathead biscuits, grits, bacon, sliced tomatoes, and a large mug of hot coffee.

He knew the General would not eat. So, he devoured his food instantly and without remorse while waiting. He borrowed a copy of the Times-Daily newspaper, in order to scan the details of last nights game and quotes from the coaches and players. He also learned high-lites of news from around the nation and especially local information.

He looked up at the glass paned French doors to see the General standing outside gazing through and looking with eye contact. He was wearing casual civilian clothing and nothing amiss. He entered and walked over straight to the judge and shook his hand with each man showing friendly smiles. To the outsider this would seem as if another civilian attorney there to meet with the judge or just another businessman.

They chatted a bit and finally stood and walked out but stopped as Billy Ray's former teammates quizzed him about last night's game and were taken back as they learned Billy Ray had not gone to the game. Heidi and he had visited the synagogue in Florence for food and hospitality. It was a format they had worked out upon their marriage vows. It had been an enjoyable evening. In lieu of the tormented life she had experienced it was so little he had to pay.

Once they were outside and away from hearing distance, the General began. "Coleman, I've been called back in due to a problem that J. Edgar is about to get involved with but before he does, Mr. Truman wants some immediate answers. It involves us, you and me.

"How and when" asked Coleman?

"It happened here." Replied the General. "Sir, what does here mean?"

"Right here in Tuscumbia."

"Best you be a little more explicit sir?"

The General answered very straight forward, "How well do you know Coach Howard?"

"Very well sir, but why do you ask?"

Silence. They continued walking in an easterly direction before Coleman took the lead and crossed the street.

"General, maybe you need to clear all of this up. Especially the part about the coach."

"Okay"

Long pause and then information flowed like a spillway at Wilson Dam opened. It's this way. Back when you were going through training in the Poconos something happened here in Tuscumbia that was not known for a period. First though, let me remind you that while we were going through the plans of capturing the Nazi, T.V.A. was omitted from a lot of the information. Reason we learned later was the management of the authority was highly jeopardized. The F.B.I. was specifically and totally involved and did not pass on to the President of the events. Upon learning bits and pieces, Mr. Truman, not liking J. Edgar very much, called me in to find out more. I was so busy at the time I'm afraid neglected too much and now "the cat is out of the bag" and Hoover is trying to find fault with all of us including you. And furthermore, not to allow the O.S.S. to be rerouted into a new service named central intelligence agency (aka C.I.A.) In addition, those T.V.A. top people could also be in "cahoots" with the Russians.

The two of us must render ourselves in this investigation as knowledgeable people. We will answer only to the President. You will be domestic investigator and I will be prone to use my connections in Europe. We will meet once a month in Washington to go over facts and figures. I know your reserve clause and will allow you to be free to do this work and of course, I am aware your term as probate judge is nearly over and I assume you will not run for re-election. Your pay increases two-fold and more to come if you are included in the C.I.A."

"What if I don't want to be included in this investigation?" questioned Billy Ray.

General retorted,

"Nobody is forcing you to do this. Know this though,"

"President Truman knows a lot about you. He was present when Mr. Roosevelt presented you with those bag full of badges and medals. Mr. Truman can re-draft you if he desires. It would be an understatement to say he is highly desirous of your involvement."

"When do you want an answer?"

"ASAP"

"You still haven't answered my question about coach Howard. How does he play in this scenario?"

They walked back to respective automobile and departed in different directions. Donovan, traveling toward Courtland in an east direction and Billy Ray going west toward Pride's Landing. They circled back and met again under the bridge going over the Tennessee river where the "nuts and bolts" were explained.

General explained, "Well it is this way. The primary person is a Mr. Robert Napier who lived next door to the coach. Together they had planned on building a type of automated football tackling dummies. Suggest you contact coach Howard and learn as much as possible about their relationship and where Mr. Napier is located now. Upon learning as much as possible, call me immediately."

The next day, Billy Ray and coach Howard, after church, played golf together. Sunday night he called Donovan with some news.

CHAPTER
FORTY-EIGHT

General Donovan was expecting the call but not this soon. Billy Ray realizing that the golf match was an important tryst and not a frivolous game. Information revealed was that Mr. Napier and coach Howard had built a four -square tree house in an area near their back porch.

It was assumed it would be for their sons to play in, but coach Howard's sons were being disciplined and not allowed to go up the tree. Napier's son also was forbidden to climb up to there so Mr. Napier told the coach he would use the facility as a storage bin. Coach Howard had built a cabinet making shop just under the high lift structure. The two men joined as partners in the shop to construct mechanical tackling "dummies" with Napier building the electrical components and Howard the physical parts. The two men would patent the construction and sell it to Wilson sporting goods for distribution. Nothing never materialized due to one Sunday night a large black automobile parked in front of the Napier home late at night and after a short time four men in black suits entered and led Napier to the auto and quickly drove away.

The next morning a moving van truck packed up all the Napier furniture and household goods and moved the family away without the father. Howard noticed when he got home from football practice a tall ladder was leaning against the tree and realized someone had entered the tree house and removed all electrical components.

No one ever found out what happened to the family. Howard

learned later that the rumor in Tuscumbia was T.V.A. terminated Napier and his family was never heard from again. The house was sold to another T.V.A. management person but nothing else materialized.

Donovan had files pulled from T.V.A., political departments, and using support from the President, the F.B.I. but to no avail. It was as if Napier ever existed. The General felt nothing much would be revealed domestically but something could be shown from the extinguished Nazi party. He knew though he'd need Coleman to join him in Berlin and London, he must bring his wife along. Heidi was overjoyed when Billy Ray told her he was taking her back home to learn about her family.

Billy Ray made advancement in the Nazi files and uncovered a character that resembled the personality of Robert Napier. Strangely this person was not German but English and had been educated at Georgia Tech University in Atlanta, Georgia. His major was electrical engineering. Even stranger, he had no family. No portraits were found and no evidence of incarceration. ANYWHERE.
The tie-in with the F.B.I. and T.V.A. was what they must seek foremost. Plus, where was Napier should he be alive or if that is his real name. The person from Georgia Tech was named Mille, and never hired by T.V.A.! Donovan used his contacts at Scotland Yard to work with Billy Ray in this undercover. Importance led to association with the communist party by whomever this person was. Complaisant to anyone trying to abhor something as atrocious as the communist party was fulfilled by law enforcement during this time. Billy Ray felt confident should he diligently give his all.
But how?

CHAPTER

FORTY-NINE

First, he must settle Heidi at her former home in Munich. The located cousin, Deni, was so glad to see her thinking all the time she was dead after being extemporaneously taken away by the Nazi ruffians in the Jewish ghetto. Her magnificent looks helped but she misbehaved and was punished by a German colonel who sent her to live with a spy in America. Since she was such a survivor doing that Billy Ray did not worry too much.

She saw him off at the military airport as he gave her a bundle of money to live on before he returned from London, hopefully with a case solved. She returned to live with her cousin and to renew some of her life working at the synagogue.

To Billy Ray, it was like old times. On a cutter in the coast guard while serving in Korea, it was constant reaction to the enemy. Now it would be research with strangers from Scotland Yard. At least they had a person of interest that was a spy to start with.

He was assigned an officer's bachelor living apartment on Cambridge University campus and posed as a professor. His colleague, Peter had already done most of the foot work. It was left up to him for verification. He conferred often with heir Napier, also known as Mille but did not allow any information out. However, heir Napier (Mille) detected his dialect and knowledge that he was from the South and point blank asked him was he from Alabama. With a smile he nodded and from that time on the culprit became more open.

The background he possessed also gave way to being the interlocutor between Billy Ray and various detectives involved in the case. They resented in allowing him to interview the communist. This was because of the comments they had heard from him previously and Billy Ray had not.

Finally, one day, the Scotland Yard people were told that he would not give out any more information to them but would to Billy Ray only. He agreed to allow recordings made during the conversations Upon hearing what had ben said, Billy Ray asked for an immediate conference with him. It was granted! Later, for a short appearance , Billy Ray spoke to him one-on-one without anybody listening and was recorded on a pocket tape recorder in the pocket of his coat when he spoke.

"Sir, what is your real name."

"Ober Mille"

"Thought it was Robert Mille?"

"Only in America"

"Did you ever work for a government organization named T.V.A.?

"Yes"

"and you were an electrical- -engineer" and

"are you aware that if you are convicted in the United States as a spy, you could be executed yet here in Great Britain your life would be spared?"

"Yes"

"Then why?"

"Here you could be convicted without much proof but in America it takes a lot of proof and not just hear-say. I could be released there but sentenced to life in prison in this country."

"Do you have a barrister?"

"No that is why I prefer to be tried in the states."

"Have you been offered someone to become your barrister? Do you want me to assist you with this?"

"No, your very gracious, but no. "

"Why?"

"Communist party in the United states will handle this."

"Very well, but I hope you know what you're doing."

Billy Ray nodded and departed. Back at his office he replayed the tape, rewound, and asked to visit with the officer in charge but first must place a call to General Donovan.

After explaining all that occurred in his visit, Billy Ray heard something he did not expect from his mentor. "Stay there, do what you are doing to the best of your ability. I'll take care of the extradition. This is for two reasons ! One , if the F.B.I. collect him he'll never make it the court room. Second, the English, for what ever reason or need, would like to convict him which in our courts, would fight this because nothing could be accomplished. The Russians would like to make another deal with J. Edgar Hoover, and this would bring about another fiasco. This is a C.I.A. matter due possibility of Hoover breaking laws and creating a lot of publicity."

"General, you know Napier only wants me to interview him. How must I deal with the folks at Scotland Yard and their political hierarchy about this situation?"

"I'll set it up with Prime Minister Harold McMillan to allow you to only meet with him. He is a conservative and pro-American and for what we did for them in Korea and World War two, this is a "small potato deal". Phone me back tomorrow from our embassy. In the meantime, meet only with the highest officer in charge and tell him what you know and play your tape to him only."

He did this much to the chagrin of Mr. Smith-Gibson. Once political wheels began turning, it was easier for him to collect evidence and interviews from Mr. Mille and it was beneficial. Scotland Yard relented and walked away. Donovan sent four agents to guard and protect Mille in route to his court dates. He was jailed in a brig at Camp Gipson, New Jersey. The trial was surprising in that the press did not care to blow anything out of proportion .

Billy Ray flew over as the chief witness for the prosecution and it was a federal matter. The defense was held together by a international attorney from Bulgaria named Toi Kline. In the eyes of the people attending the proceeds, this man was terrible. As one man explained, "he ain't no Perry Mason."

He was sentenced to be executed by firing squad at a designated military post. Billy Ray returned to London and finished up there with Mr. McMillan. His last day before he departed to Germany, he decided since Heidi had many of friends and family living on the Greek coasts, they should take a cruise on one of the new ocean liners that Mr. Ari owned so he made necessary arrangements.

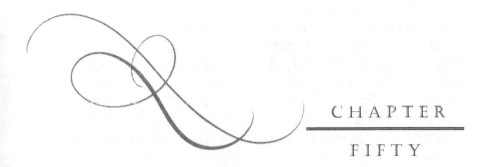

CHAPTER

FIFTY

Heidi felt so lost. Her relationship with Billy Ray now strained. To Heidi, he was just a caretaker and she needed more plus he must be Jewish German and to display the personalities of men she had known before Billy Ray. In her fantasy world every diminished people and events about them was yesterday diminutive today ingloriously enormous.

Correcting this problem required much help and it would be with her recent Rabbi, Bernard Swartz. The one man that her husband showed jealousy.

The Rabbi too, was smitten by the charms of Heidi but was married to a wonderful lady. Heidi presented herself to him once to procreate and it worked. She was having his child which proved she wasn't barren and Billy Ray was. To Heidi, the effects of love died a long time ago. Having to live with Sergeant Amis coupled with fear of losing her family gave her such proclivity regarding her loses that when Billy Ray came through and saved her from prison, she didn't understand his kindness and love.

Billy Ray had a dilemma other than his wife. Information via Scotland Yard told him a strange tale that included a trade of a German spy and a captured Russian traitor by Mr. Hoover.

Verification was needed so bad that he remained in London and Heidi staying with her cousin in the Bavarian hillside farm. Not a solution for either but financially a lifetime salary and the health insurance plan that was guaranteed couldn't be ignored. The absence from each other

couldn't be ignored either. He had not spoken to Heidi since their arrival
and of course knew nothing of his wife's condition

Through his friend, Peter Neil Jackson, an interview was arranged
with an engineer that met the requirements set forth about Mr. Napier.
Billy Ray was ecstatic. If he could get this case settled, he would begin
settling his marriage and what infidel caused what was "eating" Heidi.
He had planned a Greek cruise on a new luxury liner and visit many
of the places she had visited as a child. He thought this would be the
starting place for them.
That night in the rain clouds of London, Billy Ray phoned her from a
short wave set up in his office asking "Hi honey, how are you?"

'I am o.k., where are you?"
"In the rainiest city in the world. I miss our home and the singing
river."
"Yes, me too, but is nice to be in Bavaria again. Just to hear
people speaking in my birth language plus Yiddish is a treat."
"Heidi, I maybe finishing up here early. Thought WE could go on
a Greek tour on one of those luxury liner- ships for a week before we go
back home"

There was a long pause before Heidi spoke again and said "Billy
Ray, this is my home now, so many memories have come back and I
now realize I'm a Jewish German and I'll never be a protestant southern
belle. I think we'll divorce."
"Do you have enough money to live on for a while,'
"Didn't you hear! I want a divorce!"
"No, and you are a southern belle."
"Well, send me two hundred dollars now and when you finish
your tasks, I'll meet you in Munich at the Ambassador hotel. Meantime
I will see my barrister and ask him to file necessary papers and I'll have
our divorce papers with me.
"Why are you doing this ? When we were in Alabama you told
me how much you loved me and now this. Have you another man? Is it
your Rabbi? Just explain to me why! Why!
"Very well you can't Father a child"
"Explain that?"
"Because I think I am pregnant and yes, it is his. We were
intimate one evening and doing the Math, it could not be yours. I want

172

him and not you even though you have been good to me, I need a child a Jewish German child. As often as we tried I never got pregnant . I wanted your baby so bad! And you could not give me one. I was wrong going to bed with him, but you left me alone here with a man that showed me attention."

Another long pause then Billy Ray spoke up, "Heidi I will give you a divorce in order to dissolve what I thought was terrific but now I see you cared nothing for me. You just wanted me to provide for you. I will meet you in Munich with MY divorce papers. I shall divorce you on grounds of infidelity. Shame on you Heidi!" He then hung up the short wave and wept.

Barnard's wife shot and killed him when he told her of his intentions. The man interviewed was in fact Mr. Napier, nee Robert Green. He confessed everything including the family that posed as his. In reality, a paid immigrant group that now lived in Canada. In the tree house was stored a lot of short -wave instruments including where an enigma was place evidence found there was sent to the F.B.I. He got his job with the T.V. A. through some suppliers that bribed for his employment. They were members of the American Nazi party. Later he was tried and executed in America, because in the endeavors he was revealed as a spy. Nothing he did however, proved the folks he was involved with ever diminished the efforts of the American war efforts. As a matter of fact, T.V. A, joined in with the military and established one of the greatest law enforcement units in history. Heidi died in 1959 from venereal disease that she contacted as the top prostitute in Amsterdam.

Billy Ray returned to Alabama, sold his house and properties, bought a yacht moored in San Diego and with a small crew traveled the South Pacific and Australia and wrote of his association with the United States Coast Guard. He returned to Korea for a visit but never to the Gulf of Mexico or Europe . The wars were over for him. Politics never really interested him nor marriage again. He settled in the old home place at PRIDE'S LANDING.

Gerald "Jerry" Adams

About Gerald "Jerry" Adams:

Jerry, retired Athletic Supervisor, Coach and lecturer, grew up in the Northwest area of Alabama. Graduated from School of Sports Management North Carolina State University, Nashville Film institute, Dov Simons Film Producer's School.

Jerry also has one daughter, Angie Tomlinson, son Mike Adams, Wife Connie and five grand-sons.

CPSIA information can be obtained
at www.ICGtesting.com
Printed in the USA
JSHW080039080323
38618JS00001B/15